For My Father Carl
white water rafting on waves of light
in the ascended realms

ACKNOWLEDGEMENTS

I wish to thank my friends Jerry Hill and Beatrice Rusie for their support, suggestions and encouragement throughout this process. They have been especially helpful in providing guidance when this book needed to go to a higher level.

I wish to thank my son Justin, who put the original hand written manuscript into the computer for me, so I could work on it from there.

Finally, I wish to thank my wife Sandy, who proof-read the final copy and helped to improve the final text. I also wish to thank her for her support and encouragement as I worked on this book over several years.

Introduction

I have written a book that is thoughtful, inspirational, and readable, examining basic truths in a practical, direct and easy to understand manner. The book is about approaching life with an adventurous attitude, seeing all events and experiences as opportunities for learning, growth and increased awareness at the physical, mental, emotional and spiritual levels. The book explains how all of life has meaning and purpose, and that in meeting all of life's challenges, true happiness and joy emerge.

I was inspired by events and experiences in my life journey, as well as the events and experiences of others. My experience as a psychologist, and the events and experiences of my clients, further add to the process of understanding and making sense of life on this planet, at this point in time and space.

The book is about personal growth and spiritual development. It is about healing for individual well-being that ultimately speaks to collective healing for global well-being. The book explores topics that range from the concept of serendipity, to how to walk the path of joy. It is based on the premises that we are spiritual beings having a human experience, that we live in a lawful universe, that planet Earth is a classroom, that the purpose of life in this classroom is to become increasingly aware while experiencing the physical dimensions, and that we create our own reality by how we think and how we use spiritual truth. The book explores how we can return to our true self so that we can become Co-Creators with God. The book is equal parts psychological, philosophical, metaphysical, and spiritual. It begins with the premise that life is adventurous, ready to offer each person the experiences and challenges they need for their growth and development, and ultimately for their spiritual unfoldment. Allowing an adventurous attitude to govern life, one is able to approach the myriad experiences, events and challenges of life in a fresh, new and opportunistic manner.

Ultimately, I have written this book to share how the path of joy can be manifested in our lives, so that we can create our lives as masterpieces of joy.

I take a fresh look at the basic, or universal, truths or principles of life, examining them as these apply to creating joy. The book is divided into two sections, the first about understanding basic truths to create joy, and the second to apply basic truths to create joy.

In the first part of the book I explore the concept of serendipity, painful realities everyone must face, general and specific lessons we encounter in life, understanding universal laws such as the law of karma, the law of grace, and reincarnation, the sense of mission each of us can come to know, and how to understand what God's plan is for us. Each of these areas is examined as it helps each of us create joy through an adventurous attitude of exploring and understanding how these principles operate in our lives.

The second part of the book examines how applying universal principles creates joy. I share how my own experience with provocative neighbors becomes transformed as I move from vindictive reactions to a proactive approach using positive, healing technologies and affirmative responses.

I then explore how right thought, having an attitude of gratitude, sharing love, living from the heart, and being of service can be put into action in our lives, not only to enrich ourselves but to heal humanity and the planet as well.

I close the book by providing guidance and ways of practical application to enhance growth, increase awareness and be purposeful in our approach to life. I speak to the process of creating joy and happiness, through self-healing with an adventurous spirit, as we face all the events, challenges and adversities life has to offer. Finally, I emphasize how the path to joy is about returning to our true self, the Higher Self within each of us, that is the spiritual being having the human experience.

I have written a book that re-examines basic principles, or truths, as they apply to creating joy. I am integrating many basic truths to show how to enter the path of joy, so that you can make your life a masterpiece of joy.

PART ONE

UNDERSTANDING BASIC TRUTH

TO CREATE JOY

CHAPTER ONE

LIFE IS . . .

Life is a grand and glorious adventure. It is meant to be lived with joy, excitement and enthusiasm. Even adversity and challenge are wonderful opportunities when met and faced with a sense of ultimate discovery. As we create joy in our lives, as we create our lives as masterpieces of joy, we live adventurous and fulfilling lives.

Life is an adventure in discovering, creating and manifesting the path of joy. As we understand basic truths we are able to create lives of joy, and as we apply these truths we create our lives as masterpieces of joy. Creating joy requires healing at all levels —physical, mental, emotional and spiritual. With an adventurous attitude healing begins as we discover how basic truths manifest for us, and teach us what we need to know for healing to occur.

All healing is self-healing, and begins with self-love and self-worth. The adventurous approach to life creates the opportunity to choose self-healing, and ultimately to choose the path of joy. We are worthy of self-love for we are beloved creations of God. Created by Pure Love, we are already able to love ourselves, but somewhere along the way we forget how to do this or are taught we somehow are not worthy of loving ourselves. As we begin the process of self-healing at all levels, we learn to love ourselves again.

Life is filled with many remarkable events, some outstanding, and some just small, daily events hardly noticed unless we begin to be aware of them. An adventurous attitude is to be daring, to be bold, and to take risks. Whether this is speaking up for the first time, saying "no," volunteering, trying something new, or listening to your intuition, all are adventurous ways of approaching life. Become adventurous, living and seeking life in a courageous and enterprising manner.

Have you ever experienced a sense of adventure in your life? Do you experience adventure in your life at this time? or, has there been a time in your life, recently or in the past, when you had a sense of adventure?

Perhaps you recall the sense of adventure and excitement you experienced as a child when you explored a new place for the first time. Maybe there was a woods nearby, with paths along a stream or to a clearing or to a hill overlooking the area. Maybe you found a cave with friends, explored the inside, feeling as though you were the first discoverers of that wonderful place. Perhaps adventure came when you went hiking or camping, stayed at a lake or seashore, or traveled with your family to a different place.

Perhaps adventure was found in your imagination as you created something new, solved a problem, learned how to fix or build something, or through a book. Maybe books of discovery, adventure, exploration and mystery fired your imagination. Hopefully, adventure was sometimes found at school when new areas of knowledge opened to you.

Perhaps adventure came as an adult when you visited a new place or a foreign country. Perhaps you felt the wonder of adventure as you learned how to drive a car, or the first time you were able to take the car out on your own. Maybe the feeling of adventure came to you the first time you kissed the first love in your young life, or maybe the adventure happens over and over again as you love the significant other in your life.

Is adventure still a part of your life? Do you still experience a sense of adventure and wonder when you travel, particularly when visiting a place that you have longed to see? Does an action-adventure movie still excite you? Does watching an Indiana Jones movie rekindle the sense of adventure you have experienced in other times or places? Or, does going on a cruise to exotic ports bring a sense of adventure into your life?

Who hasn't experienced a wondrous sense of adventure when visiting Disney World? From the moment you arrive and see the characters ready to greet you, to all the exciting and entertaining experiences the Disney people know all too well how to present, your visit becomes the perfect experience of adventure and remains fondly remembered for years to come. Perhaps adventure is experienced at work or play, in trying a new job or learning a new sport.

Adventure in our lives does not have to be limited to the special events or happenings that occur from time to time, nor something as exotic as a Safari vacation in Africa. Adventure does not have to be limited to the vicarious action of a movie or novel. Nor does it have to be limited to an occasional foray to a new ethnic restaurant.

Life itself can be, and is, an on-going adventure. Adventure is an attitude, an approach, to life and all of its experiences and challenges. The most precious gift of all, from God, is the most exciting, grand and wonderful adventure we can experience. For as we meet, face and handle each moment and each challenge, we become increasingly aware of our purpose, meaning and role in life, and gain from life what life in the physical dimension is trying to teach us. Instead of being a victim, or reacting to life's challenges, we can actively benefit by using life's events to enter the path of joy.

The dictionary defines adventure as an exciting experience, a hazardous enterprise, or as a bold and dangerous undertaking of uncertain outcome. Life can certainly be an exciting experience, filled with risks and the unknown. Adventure is also defined as a remarkable occurrence in our personal history. A noteworthy event or experience in our life can, and often does, happen unexpectedly. To risk or hazard, to take a chance, to venture on, sometimes just to attempt is to be adventurous. An adventurer attempts or takes part in bold, novel, or extraordinary enterprises. Since life itself is an extraordinary enterprise, why not approach it with an attitude of adventure.

Life certainly begins as an adventure. Anyone watching a toddler exploring his/her world with wonderment and joy sees the adventurous approach in action. Watching my son learning how to crawl for the first time, persistently pulling himself up on all fours, going backwards before he figured out forwards, reminded me of the exhilaration that comes from learning how to do something. From there it was only a short, daring process to pull himself up and begin to take those tenuous initial steps. Young children have that sense of excitement, discovery and joy that Jesus reminded us was the state of mind we needed to re-enter in order to learn and apply truth in our lives. The path of joy a child naturally expresses can be returned to as an adult through an adventurous attitude.

Oftentimes the adventure comes in being ready for, and aware of, the small moments of joy and sharing. When my son was eleven years old he played Little League football. He played cornerback on the defensive unit and his job was to turn a play in to the middle of the field and not let the running back get outside of his position on the field. On one play he came in toward the runner, who was able to get around him and down the sideline for a big gain. His coach took him aside and instructed him on what to do next time.

I happened to be on the sideline for the game, as the coaching staff needed someone to keep track of playing time for each player. It was my first time on the sideline and when my son came near, he avoided me, partly because of his age and partly because he had not done well.

Later in the game, the opposing team attempted the same play. My son was ready, turning the runner in toward the middle of the field, and then catching him from behind and, almost singlehandedly, tackling the ball carrier. Oh! The joy on his face as he came off the field and found me to share his triumph. What a great adventure for me to share this moment with him, aware in the moment. If he never accomplishes another thing in sports, we will have experienced an extraordinary event together. It will not matter what else does or does not occur in sports for him. The adventure of that one moment in time will endure forever.

Sometimes the sense of adventure emerges in such unexpected ways, just by being aware something special is happening. I attended the funeral of a colleague's husband who suddenly became ill and quickly died from cancer. I was a little reluctant to go at first, not being real excited about attending funerals anyway. I tried rationalizing to myself the church was in a bad neighborhood, not being fond of funeral masses, and not knowing the deceased personally. Yet I decided to go, not only to honor him, but also to honor his wife and her love and devotion to him. Am I ever glad I went! What a wonderful adventure the experience became, even in the midst of such sadness and pain.

St. Elizabeth Roman Catholic Church is on the near East side of Detroit, in an impoverished area of the city. The area is bleak, with run-down homes, empty lots, boarded up and burnt out buildings. There seems to be little life in the neighborhood and it seems devoid of joy.

Victor lived his adventure and expressed his love of God by being the musical director of this church, as well as teaching music and religion in the Catholic school system. Victor was an accomplished musician who played for numerous churches throughout his career and was respected as a leading Gospel musician in the Detroit area.

St. Elizabeth is a one hundred eight-year-old parish that originally served a predominantly Polish area. It has adapted to the changes in the neighborhood, reflecting the largely African-American congregation it serves. The African colors and a Black Jesus adorn the altar and priestly vestments, even as the original artwork and statues adorn the church.

As the family entered the church and closed the casket, the organ music changed from somber funeral music, gradually becoming more lively and jazzy. One suddenly became aware the choir had risen and was gently swaying to the music. The choir was all black, except for two white elderly ladies who were members of the parish for years. They, too, adapted becoming active, participating members of what now was a Gospel choir.

The funeral lasted two hours, combining traditional and African-American features. Open praying of thanks for Victor, shouts of "amen", and clapping and raising one's right arm to respond to the revivalistic questions of the priest added to the sad, yet joyous, celebration of his life. All faiths worshiped together, celebrating Victor's life. What a joyous experience celebrating together, accepting differences and yet experiencing unity. Think what the world would be like if this happened all the time, for part of the larger adventure is to learn, accept and enjoy the diversity of humankind, ethnically, racially, culturally and spiritually.

Sometimes the adventurous approach is required when we face a great challenge, especially when there is injustice. A friend of mine worked hard on his recovery from drugs and alcohol, living an abstinent life style and actively involved in AA and NA. He also grew spiritually, becoming actively involved with his church and others.

When he was young and heavily addicted, he committed armed robberies to finance his addiction. Eventually he ended up in prison. On one Christmas Eve, making a Christmas tree out of bits of scrap paper with cellmates, he vowed he would turn his life around, get clean from his addictions and reform his life.

He did indeed transform his life, married and became an addictions therapist. Unfortunately, his adolescent step-daughter accused him of sexually harassing her. He claimed his innocence but was charged, with the aid of a police lieutenant who was very good friends with the natural father. It appears my friend was persecuted by this policeman, who even tried to get the media involved.

Due to his previous felony conviction, the circumstances were poor that he would be able to defend himself and, even the presumption of innocence until proven guilty would be difficult to present to a jury. A plea bargain agreement was reached and he had to return to prison. This was certainly not the kind of adventure, adversity or challenge he expected or wanted.

The first night he was back in prison, as the cell door closed behind him and he was all alone, he shared how he prayed that he would be "worthy to face the challenge God placed before me." He prayed he would live up to the ideals he believed in and lived since his life was transformed. He said to God, "I don't know why You have placed me in this situation, but I am not going to fail." He determined he would stay joyous, positive and create good.

It was difficult, but he succeeded. The reality of prison is one must live in constant vigilance. Prisons are cauldrons of fear, hate, racial antagonism and violence that dehumanize everyone. Imagine a place where your life is worth only two packs of cigarettes. Imagine a place where if you assert yourself to keep younger prisoners from harassing older ones, you can be marked for revenge by angry young gangs. Imagine a place where you are automatically labeled "bad" no matter who or what you are, and a place where authorities feel justified in not following the rules, including the parole rules.

Despite all this my friend put his beliefs into action. He

participated in and facilitated recovery support groups, developed and implemented substance abuse treatment programs, and eased tensions and provided understanding and healing between prisoners and corrections officers.

The recommendations from prison staff and treatment professionals were so glowing, the parole board decided he should serve more time, because he didn't fit the stereotype and because they didn't think he was sufficiently punished nor suffered enough in their minds from the prison experience. It took six more months to get out, by suing the Department of Corrections. Although the experience was painful, and it took months for the stress to disappear from his face and body, he didn't lose his idealism or his belief system. His joy and his positive mental attitude remained.

His challenge became an opportunity "to walk the walk" and put into action an adventurous attitude. My friend said the long-timers and corrections officers could not figure him out, because he had an old number, yet acted with enthusiasm and grace, not hardened and bitter. While in prison, he worked hard to forgive his step-daughter, the lieutenant and the father.

His wife lived her own adventure of standing by him, working on her own forgiveness of those who tried to take her husband away.

Adventure is in facing the great challenges of life in the day-to-day, moment-by-moment, here-and-now events in our lives. It is not always easy to do, especially when we have been victimized by life and when injustice occurs. However, remaining a victim is a choice, leading only to unhappiness, fear and resentment. The adventurous attitude will help in overcoming adversity, although there is no shortcut through painful events in our lives.

My friend shared one special moment on a Sunday morning shortly after he arrived in prison. A group of prisoners worshiped in the cell-block, in a place surrounded by tiers of cells. They began to sing the hymn "Amazing Grace" and, before long, were joined by all three hundred prisoners in that cell-block. My friend stated, "I knew in that moment all of us are blessed by God and never forgotten." He knew he was not abandoned, even facing the greatest challenge and testing he or anyone might ever be called upon to experience.

Big challenges or small, adversity or triumph, daily tasks or special events—all are opportunities to live an adventurous life. Adventure is an attitude, an expection, an approach to life and its many challenges. In meeting and facing all challenges, and in appreciating all that we experience, we learn and grow. Most of all, in facing the challenges and not avoiding them or trying to sidestep them, we ultimately experience joy and happiness.

Many argue that the only two things certain in life are death and taxes. To this I would add a third certainty, we will get challenges. The process of meeting, greeting and dealing with the challenges counts as much as arriving at the destination. So, as the procession of life unfolds, be adventurous and find joy in the process.

In October, 1993 I was suddenly diagnosed with adult-onset diabetes. I had no idea this challenge was coming into my life and I was chagrined to learn it was happening, to say the least. Blood work was redone, and the diagnosis was confirmed. The first night, as the reality of my physical situation set in, I had a vivid dream in which I was being locked into a drab, gray prison cell, with a heavy metal, barred door closing behind me. It was one of those dreams in which the conscious mind is aware of the dream and its interpretation, even as one sleeps soundly. I "knew" my life was changing and I would not longer be able to live the lifestyle, regarding food, I previously enjoyed. I also "knew" I had a choice to meet the challenge or be imprisoned by the experience that entered my life.

The next two weeks I suffered from grief and loss as I let go of the fats and sugars I had grown to love so dearly. A physician friend and colleague was sought out for advice on how to proceed in meeting this new challenge in my life, the physical disease that was now a reality I had to deal with. A recovering drug abuser, now active in recovery support groups, he congratulated me on my situation. He told me, "This is the best thing that could ever happen to you!" He said it laughingly and positively, knowing that this new reality would prompt me to become healthier, eat better, and take better overall care of my health and physical needs. It was not said with malice.

At the time I was diagnosed with diabetes I was considerably overweight. I weighed 247 pounds, down only slightly from an all-time high of 260. Although I was running four to five miles per day, I was hardly in ideal physical shape.

While I am in the business of helping others to face and change destructive and unhealthy patterns and choices, I don't always apply those principles to myself. Foremost in the process of healing, no matter at what level the healing has to take place, is that all healing begins with self-love and self-worth.

While my self-esteem has generally been good, it was time to allow total self-love and self-worth into my life. It is harder to love ourselves than it should be, but the emotional scars of a lifetime often take their toll on our self-esteem. At some point we have to make the choice to heal these scars and move toward total self-love.

Further, I had to develop a plan of action to restore health to my body, a plan that addressed healing at all levels-physical, mental, emotional and spiritual. I had to develop and implement a physical regimen which would lead to weight-loss and would include exercise. My physician friend told me if I lost fifty pounds, significantly reduced fat and sugar from my diet, and exercised regularly, my body would not require additional insulin to reduce the sugar level in my body.

I began a program of healthy eating which continues to this day. It took a month for my body to adjust to significantly reduced sugar and fat intake and for my taste buds to change so that natural sugars in fruits would be appealing. Now if I try to eat a piece of cake, like I recently tried to do at a birthday party, all I can taste is the fat. It is like eating pure grease. As I have modified my eating pattern, I feel better and weight has come off. Nine months later, due to the change in my diet and due to exercise, I now weigh 210 pounds and I continue to gradually lose more weight.

Part of the plan of action was to run daily, and increase the amount of mileage, to further facilitate weight loss and to burn excess sugar in my body. I also had a long-standing dream to run in a marathon. At the end of May, 1994 I was ready to begin a twenty week training program so I could run in the Detroit Free Press International Marathon scheduled for October, 1994.

Twice before I tried to train for this, once falling short of my goal and once becoming ill late in the training program and unable to regain my strength in time to run in the race.

In October, 1994, I ran in the Detroit Free Press/Mazda International Marathon, completing all 26.2 miles in four hours and thirty-four minutes. Determination with the training paid off. I had to run 45 to 50 miles per week to increase endurance. The physical healing the diabetes required also helped me achieve a goal which eluded me at a younger age.

Healing at the mental level meant I had to choose and accept a new concept for myself. Since mind is the builder and what we think is what we create for ourselves, I had to change my mental outlook to better meet this challenge. In consultation with a trusted, psychic advisor, I came to understand my diabetes was more in thought form than in physicality. If I worked on healing at the mental level, it would eventually cease to be a reality in my life.

I also learned from another "angelic" source I had placed the genetic encodement for diabetes in my DNA structure as a "hurdle," to help awaken me to my true Divine heritage and my mission and purpose in life. As a result of this challenge, tremendous growth and increasing awareness occurred in just one year, as I received my "wake-up call" to larger wisdom and truth, and the manifestation of the same in my life and in my work with others. I moved even more into a life of service. However, it all had to begin with and continue to include self-healing. Other people only act as guides or facilitators in the healing process.

All healing, including emotional healing, begins with self-love and self-worth. I had to change my relationship with food—to stop using food for my emotional needs. It was not unlike an alcoholic who often uses alcohol to address feelings of depression, anxiety or fear.

Finally, I had to address spiritual healing, as I began to forge a greater understanding and awareness of my relationship with God. Out of this has emerged the development of a true partnership with God, in which I increasingly align my will with His Will. I have begun to meditate on a daily basis, seeking my connection with God and opening myself up to His guidance and gentle reassurance of my connection with Him. I have also learned to listen more often to the "still, small voice within" which intuitively guides me to the best choices and courses of action in my life, on a daily basis. Freely choosing to create a genuine partnership with God allows me to heal at all levels, to become increasingly aware, and to provide service in accord with the Divine Plan and my mission and purpose.

As a result of my health challenge, the spirit and attitude of adventure have grown. In just one year, tremendous healing has begun. My professional life has advanced tremendously as I learn and implement new healing technology, and add my experience to the process of guiding others to their own self-healing.

When the Reverend Jack Boland, Senior Minister of the Church of Today, a Unity church in Warren, Michigan, was dying of cancer, he taught all of us a wonderful lesson in his choice of an adventurous approach and attitude toward life, even as life was slipping away from him. He approached his cancer with joy and enthusiasm, at first fighting that dreadful disease, later accepting that the cancer would triumph over him. He rarely gave into despair that life was coming to an end for him. As his time on Earth came to an end he held onto life, not out of fear for what was coming next, but to finish work he knew he needed to complete.

One task he worked on was fully forgiving his mother, knowing he needed to complete this work, before he was ready to move back into spirit. As his organ systems were shutting down at the end, and he could no longer eat or drink, he found joy and pleasure in simply chewing on ice chips. Especially when grief was being processed with those present, he often buoyed their spirits by relieving the tension and saying, "I think I'll chew on more ice chips." He stayed light-hearted and joyful. To the end his indomitable spirit comforted the grief-stricken friends and associates around him. He died as he learned to live, with joy, enthusiasm, optimism and adventure.

A month before he died, he last attended the church he worked so hard to build and loved so dearly. A living memorial service was held with those present whom he had influenced, as well as those who had influenced him. It was a sad but moving experience which celebrated life and the adventure life can be. I would suggest to you when we approach life in the same manner, we can achieve a feeling of joy even as life is ending.

Victor, whose funeral was described earlier, suddenly developed lung cancer while on vacation. Within two weeks he was very ill and lost thirty pounds. Once back in Detroit he was immediately hospitalized and treatment began. Despite these efforts he died after two months. He was health conscious, ate the right foods and regularly exercised. He was a positive thinker with a joyful attitude. Even being African-American married to a white woman, never did prejudice result in a negative, bitter attitude. His reaction to his cancer was to remain positive and to comfort those around him.

He kept telling his wife, "Expect a miracle." He always said this to her before when adversity or misfortune affected their lives, and always in the past positive results occurred. It was not to be that way this time. Yet, as he valiantly fought the illness steadily and surely invading his body, he remained positive and optimistic.

Everyone who worked in the hospital knew about him and what a joy it was to be around him. Daily, the staff checked to see how he was doing. He truly believed he would triumph over adversity again.

While he was unable to defeat the cancer, he was able to leave his wife with one more gift. He was determined he would not die on their anniversary, even when his heart and lungs were failing and he was given twenty-four hours at best. He lived three more weeks, so his death would not be remembered on their day of joy and celebration.

During the winter months of 1994-95, the challenge of death came to me unexpectedly. While away at a party on December 10th, visiting friends I hadn't seen for a long time, I was suddenly paged by my brother. He told me a local hospital called to advise us our father was there and the family should come as soon as possible. It was all he knew.

Since I have privileges at the hospital, I called immediately expecting to hear Dad was seriously ill. Instead, the resident on duty in the Emergency Room said he died of a heart attack a short while earlier. While his health was poor, it was still a shock as there was no warning death was imminent.

Six weeks later my 43 year old brother celebrated his birthday.

The next morning he died in bed of a massive heart attack which also came without warning. Suddenly he was gone as well. While I knew I would handle these personal losses adventurously, they were still deeply painful and hard to face initially.

Of some comfort, in both situations, was the contact I was able to make, both directly and indirectly, with both of them in spirit. I had visions of my father in the spiritual realm, one of which occurred at his memorial service. One of Dad's last adventures was a trip whitewater rafting on the Colorado River through the Grand Canyon. In the vision at the memorial service, I saw him white water rafting, on waves of light, joyously laughing. I "knew" all was well with him, and it was a great comfort.

Through a friend with a special psychic ability, I also communicated with my father and learned why he left and what he had to say to me as a result. He expressed his joy at being back in spirit, and asked me not to mourn very long or be side-stepped from my mission.

As I drove to the hospital where the ambulance took my brother, I "knew" he was gone. I could hear his voice in my mind, asking me "to watch out for my wife and son," and regretting the recent conflict between us. He also stated, "I know I have to atone for my life."

That statement and especially his use of the word "atone" was very interesting, for atone was not a word he used when alive. In a latter communication, through my psychic friend, Jerry, he mentioned again he was to "atone" for his life. He also said, "I was in bed one minute and suddenly in a dark tunnel the next, wondering where I am. Tell Sharon I did not feel any pain. I came to a shimmering wall of light and, standing there, were Dad and Bob (an Ascended Master), waiting to greet me and help me in getting used to being in spirit again."

He stated he would be allowed a period of healing and relaxation, "spiritual R and R" if you will, before he would have to do his atonement. He told me his anger killed him and he had to resolve anger and its consequences in the spirit realm.

While there is some comfort for me in being able to

communicate with my deceased relatives, it has still been a painful period in my life, as I struggled to deal with grief and loss of my father and brother. It has been challenging to live with an adventurous attitude with these painful realities in my life. However, since I am living more and more with enthusiasm, and understanding these events in my life with an adventurous attitude, I am able to handle both deaths at once. With calmness I am managing grief and loss while accepting the greater truth these events bring to my life.

Wayne Dyer, noted author and psychologist, has profoundly stated the following truth, "We are spiritual beings having a human experience." Say these words aloud. Feel their impact. Certainly, we have viewed ourselves in the opposite way. We have conceived of ourselves as human beings searching for spiritual truth, and ultimately, a spiritual home or destiny.

This shift in emphasis from conceiving of ourselves as humans first to conceiving of ourselves as spiritual first is our true heritage. Thus life takes on a renewed meaning and purpose when our true nature is understood. As a spiritual being having a human experience, part of the adventure of life is to understand and apply universal truths within a human physical existence. Through the process of discovering truth, wisdom and knowledge we then come to further know our spiritual nature. The ultimate adventure is becoming fully aware of our true nature, and as we do so the path of joy naturally emerges for us.

Life throws many challenges, adversities and opportunities our way. Meeting these events and facing these presents us with many adventurous experiences. With the attitude of adventure great opportunity awaits each of us. Ultimately, we begin to experience the path of joy as understanding and applying basic truths begins to occur, allowing self-healing to manifest in our life.

The adventure is in living life to the fullest, taking advantage of all events and experiences, avoiding none, meeting all. Get excited about your adventure in discovery, healing, learning and growing.

Adopt an adventurous attitude, recapture the experience of it in your life. Although life is filled with many events, and sometimes painful realities, an adventurous approach will allow all events and situations to lead you to a greater awareness, wisdom and understanding of your true spiritual heritage, and to making your life a masterpiece of joy.

CHAPTER TWO

THERE ARE NO COINCIDENCES

One of the basic truths of life is there are no accidental occurrences. The good news is everything is happening exactly as it should in our lives! The bad news is adversity and seeming injustice also are happening exactly as they should in our lives! The latter makes it very challenging to be adventurous, but understanding this can help us to make sense of our lives and to meet the painful events in more productive and positive ways. Even if we can't always understand why certain events or situations are happening to us, understanding all is in divine order can help us to "turn stumbling blocks into stepping stones to our greater good."

This principle has been taught by Jack Boland and others, and is called the principle of serendipity. Nothing happens by chance; all unfolds according to what is needed for each individual to experience at each moment in time. We live in such an incredible universe. It continually provides us with the challenges, the experiences and the opportunities we need so we can grow, prosper, develop and become increasingly aware. The universe continually provides us with the opportunity to meet ourselves in many different situations so that we may advance physically, emotionally, mentally and spiritually.

This is a highly complex process, requiring the interaction of many laws working simultaneously. This dynamic process is further complicated by the nature of the future events which may occur. For they are only probabilities based on the free will choices we make individually and collectively. The future is not preordained, but manifests as we choose individually and collectively each day. Yet, certain experiences may seem preordained as we may have to meet certain challenges or learn certain lessons.

Additionally, when one challenge is concluded or lesson is learned, we get new challenges and lessons, especially on this planet. For as V. Michael Murphy, former Unity minister, so succinctly stated it, "We are not on this planet to have a vacation." When I first heard this I thought to myself, "You mean we don't get any breaks, we don't get to coast." Up until then I kept hoping we achieve the goal or somehow get it, and then life ceases to be a struggle. In fact, the opposite seems to be true. When we finish one lesson we get another! Guess what else? The more we grow spiritually, the more challenges we get! We are here to work, to grow, to have the human experiences in the physical realm. The more we embrace life the more life gives us.

I have observed over time there are no accidents, whether in the many events that have occurred in my life, or in the lives of others I know. I would invite you to make the same observation about your life and the lives of those around you. You will find as you watch what unfolds, and as you review your life up until now, this principle operates.

Understanding that this basic principle does operate, every seeming coincidence is actually operating for the highest good at all times, even when this does not appear to be readily apparent. When we begin to pay attention to the coincidences of our lives, we can begin to discern why these events are occurring as they do, and can begin to ask how these may be serving our greater good. If even the unpleasant events in life are present at a particular time for a reason, as I become aware of why the event is arising as it is, I can learn from the experience and can derive benefit for my greater understanding and further growth at any level. Even if I can't discern why the event is in my life, understanding this truth, I can make the best of it expecting it to indeed serve my highest good ultimately.

At one time I was working on an adolescent inpatient psychiatric unit of a suburban general hospital. There were five psychologists and five social workers who served as primary therapists for 40 patients at any one time. While patients were assigned randomly to treatment teams and therapists at the time of admission, I began to observe that almost always the adolescent and/or his family ended up with the "best" therapist they needed to help them at that point in time.

One striking example was a 16 year old male who was very artistic, sensitive and creative. He was in constant conflict and turmoil with his father, who wanted him to be more "masculine" and especially to be involved in sports. The father was constantly critical of his son for not being more manly, and tried to discourage his son's natural abilities, temperament and destiny.

Of the ten potential therapists, this patient was assigned to a male social worker very much like himself. The therapist was an accomplished jazz pianist who was gentle and sensitive in his relationships, both professionally and personally. Not only was he able to provide a meaningful role model for this young man, he was also able to guide this young man to accept and be himself. He was further able to help the father understand his son's true self, accept masculinity comes in many forms, accept his son had his own life to lead and could not be an extension of what his father wanted.

Subsequently, I worked at an outpatient psychiatric clinic, staffed by numerous psychiatrists, psychologists and clinical social workers. The clinic therapists were psychoanalytically-oriented, focusing on the particular long-term therapy approach the analytic model provides. I was, as nearly as I could tell, the only therapist more willing to utilize other treatment approaches. I also appeared to be the only one who might not regard talking about spiritual issues or paranormal experiences as a sign of abnormal emotional difficulties.

While clients were assigned on a random basis, inevitably I would have those clients needing or wanting to talk about spiritual issues, the mental and emotional aspects of physical illnesses, the effects of the law of karma and the law of grace in their lives, the possibility they had lived other lives, "deja vu" experiences, wanting to understand free will versus predestined existences, how dreams indicated future events for them or about prophecy and predictions. Now I suppose it is possible that since I am open to listening and talking about these topics with clients, they naturally talk about them with me. Yet, I believe something more was happening.

Since there are no coincidences, I believe each client who comes to me is "meant" to see me for a specific reason. Often it appears I am the "right" therapist to help them with a particular problem or issue, to help them psychologically and/or metaphysically. One client even came to me because she heard I was a "metaphysical therapist" and traditional therapy was not working for her.

Interestingly, as I became more open to psychic phenomenon and awareness, as well as broadening psychotherapy to be inclusive of these phenomena, increasing coincidences have emerged in my daily experiences as well as in my daily interactions with others.

For example, having read about angels assuming human form, I wondered if I would recognize an angel if one were present. A few weeks later I opened the door for a middle-aged woman, and as we exchanged smiles, I suddenly recognized she was an angel. Her smile broadened in confirmation of my silent realization of her true identity, and her eyes merrily twinkled as I experienced the truth of her being. While others might think I only imagined her smile was confirming my thoughts, I intuitively knew and accepted what my thoughts were telling me. We learn to trust our thoughts and our intuitive knowing when they are validated for us over time. With enough validation, we are able to generalize our knowingness into situations which can't be directly validated. Sometimes this is just called faith.

Making the moment with the "angel" even more special was the extension of kindness directed to her by opening the door and smiling, for what I read earlier suggested we should extend our love and kindness in all directions with others, for we might not know "who" really is the recipient of our behavior and emotion.

As my practice has expanded to include metaphysical treatment approaches, I have worked with several clients who subsequently learned they are angels in human form. Interestingly, they are often in the most dysfunctional families so they can serve us by taking on the most painful parts of human existence. They can then develop healing technologies for those situations or provide healing for others who live in similar circumstances. Knowing the worst, they can now be of service to others and to humanity as a whole.

These clients learn, from the "vision hypnosis" process I discovered in my practice, how they will be helping and healing others in similar circumstances. No one will be able to discount them since they have experienced the same trauma, hurt and pain while also in third dimensional reality, with the veil of forgetfulness shrouding them as they go through the same experiences.

During vision hypnosis, one of these "angels" shared th

144,000 angels in human form on the planet at this time. Interestingly, this is the number mentioned in the Book of Revelations, often misinterpreted as the limited number that will be "saved" at the end of time. Is it any coincidences this number of angels would be on the planet as an ending of time approaches, as predicted by many sources?.

In the past two years, as I worked with regression hypnosis, a new process began to evolve, which I referred to above. I was instructed in lucid dreaming to call this "vision hypnosis" or "vision hypnotherapy." It is a fascinating process in which communication is made with client's higher selves, guardian spirits, deceased relatives, ascended masters, angels and archangels. On two occasions Jesus has come to the person, and recently the Buddha also made an appearance. Sometimes clients have visions of the future for themselves or for humanity in general. One client even witnessed the birth of a new universe.

Certain clients "come" to me so I could learn how to do this. Through the emerging hypnosis, they also are "meant" to learn their true mission and purpose in this lifetime. I have assisted many in their "wake-up call" as light workers. Through seeming coincidence, every step of the way, as I learned how to facilitate this process, the right individual or experience emerged to teach me how to do this and the unlimited possibilities this healing technology brings to all of us.

As I explore metaphysical topics and psychic phenomena, events always occur shortly after I read about them affirming those topics. For instance, having heard about psychic surgeons in the Philippines, I subsequently evaluated a mother as part of a custody and visitation evaluation in a divorce case. She had taken her daughter to a psychic surgeon, out of desperation, when traditional medicine offered her no hope her daughter could be healed without scarring her significantly.

Her daughter was born with a disfiguring congenital growth on her jaw. Unable to receive help from medical authorities in the United States, she flew to the Philippines and found a psychic surgeon. She watched the surgeon put his hand in her daughter's face, remove the growth, and seal her face so only a reddened surface remained which disappeared in a few weeks. No disfigurement of her daughter's face remained, and she showed me before and after pictures of her daughter that verified her story.

Several clients have reported encounters with recently deceased relatives. An adolescent girl I worked with kept having her grandfather appear to her at the foot of her bed each night after he died. This caused her some consternation yet she welcomed him as she was very close to him. She was instructed to help her grandfather complete his transition back into the spirit realm, by telling him she loved him but he must continue into the light. After following this instruction the next night he appeared he did not return.

During vision hypnosis, some clients have deceased relatives contact them. Most deceased relatives contact clients from the spirit realm, but there are also clients who have deceased relatives who remain near the Earth plane, and who do not go in to the light. Each time we are able to assist these souls to go "across the borderline" into the light. Through the assistance of the person in the hypnotic trance, the deceased relative describes other family members already in spirit coming to help them move into the spirit realms.

In another case which didn't require hypnosis, I found a woman in my office grieving the death of her ex-husband. She came to see me by way of her employee assistance program, seeking help for her grief and to understand the "strange" experience she had shortly after his death. Serendipitously, I just heard about this kind of experience on a television program two weeks earlier.

She was particularly upset because she angrily told her ex-husband she wished he would die the last time she saw him alive. She said this because he was refusing her advice to seek medical care. He was clearly very ill, and refused to get medical attention saying he could not afford to see a doctor and that he would be alright. This occurred as he dropped off the children following his weekend visitation with them.

Not getting medical care, he died a few days later. When she learned of his death she immediately felt guilty for the way she spoke to him the last time she saw him. She still loved him, but divorced him because of his drug problem, and his inability to stop using drugs.

The phone rang an hour after she learned he was dead. It was him on the phone, even though he was dead, telling her there was no reason to feel guilty about what she had said to him as he should have heeded her advice. He also told her he understood his role in their troubled relationship, and could take responsibility for his part in the marriage not working.

He told her he loved her and the children, and would watch over them from spirit. She was greatly reassured, but feared no one would believe her. She also feared she might have become delusional, worrying about her mental health. Is it a coincidence she was "directed" to me where her experience would not be ridiculed, and where it could be validated for her that her experience was genuine? Was it a coincidence that I had a client with this experience after hearing about it with other people? I don't think so. What a wonderful, continuing adventure life is, especially when increased awareness affirms the seeming miracles and coincidental events as they happen. Even more wonderful is how so-called coincidental experiences continually confirm what a marvelous universe it is we live in.

Ironically, but not surprisingly, later on I was sharing the story of this client with my family and Mom stated she had never shared the following with us. She said when her father was hospitalized prior to his death, she received a phone call from him telling her she had better come down to see him. She immediately "knew" she had to go if she wanted to see him one more time, and to say goodbye to him.

When she arrived in Mississippi where he was hospitalized she discovered there was no phone in his room. Upon further investigation, she learned he had been too weak to leave his room, that he had not used a phone at the nursing station, no one had seen him leave his room to use pay phones in the hallway, and he didn't have money to use for pay phones even if he could have gotten to one. How did the call occur? Did he somehow muster strength to leave his room, make a call, and return without being seen? Or, did something else happen beyond the normal limits of space and time as we generally understand them? Was it a coincidence Mom had this experience, or that she shared the experience when she did?

Seeming coincidences, large and small, happen all the time.

Driving to work one day I heard on the news about the death of a 14 year old boy from a heart attack while involved in a physical altercation with a peer at school. I was surprised to recognize the name of the boy from a family I worked with two years earlier. My "still, small voice" informed me I was to visit the family at the funeral home. While I am learning to pay attention to "my still, small voice within" I was having doubts listening to this voice this time. I also rationalized to myself it was two years since I worked with the family. Despite the doubt and the last minute fear walking in to the funeral home, I was the right person the family needed to have present.

The funeral home was filled with grieving classmates, peers and relatives. The immediate family needed someone they could talk to who was not a relative or a schoolmate. I became a refuge for them, a source of strength they could use to process their feelings and strategize how they could further help the boy who was guilt-ridden about being in the fight with their son. I was the perfect person for them in their time of need. Obviously Divine Wisdom knew to direct me there that night. Given this, how is it I was more attentive that day to the news on the car radio? How is it I "knew" I needed to go see the family? How is it I was exactly what they needed at that moment in time? If there are no coincidences, as I attend to what is unfolding in my life and attend to my intuitive knowing, I will understand the serendipitous process and make the right choices to respond for the highest good of all concerned.

As I observe the events in my life I realize there are no accidents. All events appear to unfold as they are meant to be at each point in time. Again, this doesn't mean everything is predetermined and can't be altered, although some events may be destined to happen. Based on free will choices, probabilities do occur that lead us to experiencing certain events or facing certain challenges helping us to grow, become more spiritual and demonstrate to ourselves universal laws do apply.

I attended a four day seminar, the second in a series of human potential growth seminars presented by SAGE Seminars. This seminar is called Magic Maker, and is designed to address fear, and other issues, which keep us from achieving our dreams. The seminar is also designed to address the mental and emotional aspects of our being. As with all seminars, it became readily apparent the right participants and facilitators were "brought" together by the universe, to uniquely interact with each other, and to provide the experiences each of us needed to deal with blocks in our lives preventing us from achieving our full potential, as well as all of our goals and dreams.

The seminar had 81 participants. Part of the initial process required us to randomly walk around and make eye contact with each other, without speaking a word. In this way we each "found" the ideal partner, and subsequently the ideal "family" of eight we would work with during the seminar. I say found, but in truth, each of us serendipitously connected with the ideal partner to facilitate our growth and accomplish what the seminar was meant to teach. Not surprisingly, each person was paired up with an ideal partner and family.

The first task of each pair was to go to lunch together and share with the other their deepest secret. Of course, my partner and I shared very similar secrets, and were able to provide healing with each other about that issue in our lives.

An important issue in my life in need of healing was the feeling of being left out, left behind, or seemingly abandoned. Naturally, events in the seminar unfolded in such a way so I was able to address the emotional pain of this issue for me.

One of the rules of the seminar involved returning from breaks and being at a seat by the time the music stopped, after the doors opened and you re-entered the room. There were three rows of chairs in a half-circle, and several chairs were pulled back to provide an opening into the circle.

The instructions prior to one break were for families to sit together upon return. Our family entered and went down one row only to discover there were only seven chairs, leaving me without a chair, and thus left out. I began a frantic search to find a seat before the music stopped, ending up in the "entrance," hoping when the chairs were closed there would be a seat for me. The panicky feeling I was experiencing and the overwhelming sense of fear went beyond the situation in the seminar, for truly there was nothing to fear if I ended up without a seat. The situation in the seminar allowed the unresolved fear within me to surface so I could work on it. The universe, through the seminar, was giving me a very safe place to finally resolve this issue. Even so, the power of this unresolved fear within me was very great.

One of the leaders recognized the panic written across my face as the music ended. There indeed was a chair for me, but this leader came over and gently massaged my head and shoulders in reassurance I was not abandoned or left behind, and that I was safe.

This seeming coincidence, though, re-created a powerful emotional response in me which I was then able to address in the subsequent regression meditation the group was guided through. As I meditated on the issue of being left out or left behind, I systematically went back to earlier events in my life where I felt the same way. The most recent event was when I was two out of seventeen people not hired by a managed care company which won the contract from the previous company. I then went back in time through other experiences at college, in high school with peers, until childhood when I was left out in Little League and pick-up baseball games.

I went back to my earliest memory as an infant, feeling abandoned at bedtime. I remembered lying in my crib, feeling all alone in the darkened room as I looked at the light fixture I could dimly see in the faint light. I later learned this was the moment I felt abandoned by God for being back on Earth during these turbulent and challenging times of transition, even though I also knew I willingly came to be of assistance in fulfilling the divine plan.

Further regression led to fetal remembrances of feeling alone, picking up on my mother's loneliness about being in a new city without friends and support while she was pregnant for the first time. While re-experiencing the feeling of loneliness I originally interpreted as not being wanted, I simultaneously realized the larger truth my mother's loneliness did not mean I was not wanted.

Regressing further, I went to a lifetime when I was a Native American woman in the Klamath Falls region of Oregon. I had recalled parts of this life before, and "knew" I somehow felt alone and left behind while at the river. This time I was able to recall returning to the village, seeing it abandoned, and realizing it was under attack by a warring tribe. As I began to run I was shot in the back with an arrow. During the meditation, lying on my back on the floor, I felt a sharp poke in my back at the spot the arrow entered my previous body. It felt like someone poking me with their finger, but I was against the floor.

Not coincidentally, each time I go back to that lifetime I am able to recall more information, as I am "ready" to remember it. The subconscious mind and our Higher Self have great wisdom, and only give us the information we are ready to experience when it is safe for us to do so.

In a Breakthru Seminar, facilitated by it's founder Sue Myers, I returned to this lifetime once again, this time finding myself giving birth, which is real interesting to experience since I am in a male body this time. I could see myself lying on the floor of the tepee, my legs up and apart, looking to where my daughter in that life was entering the world.

I learned the full details of that life, from a loving husband who didn't always understand me, to the son and daughter I bore. I learned I was a shaman, even though this was unheard of for a woman. I remembered the tribe having difficulty understanding me, but growing to love and accept me, and allowing me to be the shaman I was destined to be in that life.

At my death, I rose above my body, looked down at my form lying on the ground, and thought what a terrible waste it was I was killed, without any understanding by the people who murdered me who I truly was.

As I rose above North America, I could see the entire continent as I faced North, with the blue Pacific ocean glistening in the sunlight to my left. I became aware of the bond I had with the Earth then, and continue to have in this incarnation. I came to understand one of the reasons I have returned is to help with her healing in the next few years.

The events of the SAGE Seminar and the subsequent Breakthru Seminar perfectly prepared me to heal the issue of being left out or left behind, healing much of the emotional fear and pain associated with feeling abandoned. They also gave me the "perfect" experiences I needed to understand my spiritual nature in this incarnation. I was able to recognize the purpose of that life, and the ties to other lifetimes and to this lifetime.

Recently I healed the remaining part of the abandonment issue, the feeling of being left behind by God, which I first felt in the crib as an infant. I was not consciously aware I felt this way. Sue Myers, an expert in the use of the muscle response testing to understand issues at the mental, physical, emotional and spiritual level, was working with me. At one point we discovered I was angry at God for my current assignment on this planet. The root cause for concern was not wanting to endure physical discomfort or pain again. Knowing I chose to come here of my own free will, I nevertheless harbored some resentment toward God, with an underlying fear of being abandoned. I was able to forgive God and to allow this issue to finally resolve itself.

In the past two years I have met people, seemingly coincidentally, who I subsequently learned I was connected with in other lifetimes, or in experiences between lives. Some of these people have become more intimately involved with me as friends and fellow adventurers in this life.

Two of these people I met at a psychiatric unit I consult with at a general hospital. It is truly fascinating to have met these two in such a place, yet this is how all three of us have become reacquainted in this lifetime. Not surprisingly, once this principle is understood, we have known each other many times not only during incarnations on this planet, but on other planets and in other dimensions as well.

In addition to renewed friendship, we are members of a healing circle we were instructed to form by higher dimensional beings. Each member who has come to the circle has been directed to us by the universe, and again not surprisingly, we have all known each other before.

The purpose of the healing circle is to provide healing, whether to ourselves, others, humanity or the planet. We also receive instruction from angels, archangels and intergalactic beings. This healing circle consists of several individuals who come together to send healing light and energy to others and to the planet. At times we work to raise the consciousness of humanity. With the latter we are told that even when three of us are working together, a difference is made in the collective consciousness of humanity. Collective prayer and affirmation does indeed make a difference. For as Jesus taught, when two or more are gathered in his name, great changes in consciousness can occur. No doubt other healing circles have also been "instructed" to form.

At the MagicMaker seminar I previously mentioned, one of the exercises I participated in was taking an "omen walk." This involved allowing myself to be "guided" to experience the message or symbol I needed at the time. After lunch, from a restaurant across from the hotel in the Bahamas where the conference took place, I began my walk.

I immediately felt a "force" occupy my body, which directed me where to go. It walked me across the street, and then across the front lawn of the hotel. Not wanting it to lead me through a group of local men waiting at the bus stop just beyond the hotel, I let fear take control and turned toward the beach, wanting to believe this was where I was being directed to go.

Immediately the feeling of the force left me. I knew I would have "to trust and allow" and let the experience unfold as it was meant to. As I turned around, the force returned to my body with a rush, led me through the bewildered Bahamians wondering at this tourist walking through the bus stop, and led me to a residential street beyond. I was led down the street to a driveway containing a two-seat Mercedes-Benz convertible, a long-standing dream car for me. While I did not interpret the omen to mean I would literally own such a vehicle in the future, although I certainly wouldn't mind owning one or being in a position where I could afford one, I did realize prosperity and abundance would manifest in my life. This has been the reality from that point forward as I have been richly blessed, not only materially, but also in all areas of my life.

Several years ago the principle of serendipity dramatically emerged in my life, illustrating how this principle works for everyone.

After attending my church for several years, my "still, small voice within" began telling me it was time to give something back in service. I wrote to the minister, stating it was "serendipity time," and I was ready to assist in whatever way I could. I received a phone call from the minister, asking me if I could meet him prior to the 9:00 o'clock service the following Sunday. When I met him, he asked if I would be interested in assisting the Y.O.U. group at the church. This is a teen group that is provided Sunday school classes, social events and support group services.

I was particularly helpful in the latter function, especially with my training as a psychologist. The teen group assists members and their friends who struggle with serious issues, from surviving in very dysfunctional families to sometimes significant emotional problems. The two leaders of the group had been praying, affirming and visualizing a solution to their need for assistance. They had also taken their need to the minister, who also asked the universe to provide the perfect solution. Is it coincidence that I "knew" to write to the minister just at the moment when their specific need could be answered by my volunteering?

At lunch with a good friend one day, he shared with me how the principle of serendipity was operating in his life. An addictions therapist, he was using a home office the last two years. He had reached the maximum potential for service and income, but lacked the resources to develop his practice further. He went to the local home office for Alcoholics Anonymous, where he ran into a county government official familiar with the high quality treatment he provides to people suffering from addictions. This person asked if he was ready to expand the scope of his services, and if he was then grant money was available to accomplish this. Other sources of support and income also began to materialize, and he knew he could move forward with his goal of expanding services to others.

He began looking for office space, and inquired about a space that seemed to be the right size and price. The very day he went to look at the space, the previous tenants, also engaged in counseling services, were moving out. The space was immediately available, and was the "perfect" space he needed. He was also the "perfect" new tenant for the landlord, as both were immediately compatible with each other. Coincidence for all involved? Am I making my point yet?

Jack Boland taught about the principle of serendipity, based on the tale of the Three Princes of Serendip. It is a tale in which the three princes set about making discoveries, seemingly coincidentally, but always exactly how and when they most needed the information each step of the way.

Serendipity is the faculty of making happy or interesting discoveries unexpectedly or by accident. Notice the emphasis on happy as well as interesting. An adventurous attitude allows us to continually make these discoveries in a world and universe in which nothing occurs by happenstance.

Even seemingly negative or destructive events contain within them the seed of our greater good. The Reverend Boland talked often of the need "to turn stumbling blocks into stepping stones to our greater good." Even seemingly negative events or adversities can ultimately be for our greater growth and development at all levels. They, too, can ultimately be happy and interesting discoveries.

The events in your life are meant to propel you forward on to the path of joy. Start making happy and interesting discoveries in your life, as you come to understand how the seemingly unexpected or accidental situations are meant for you exactly at the moment they arrive.

We live in a complicated yet lawful universe. If there are no coincidences, then we need to respond to the events which occur in our lives, searching for the deeper meaning these events have for us. With new understanding we then can make the "right choices" for ourselves so even more positive and beneficial experiences can subsequently emerge. For as we abide by truth principles, greater good comes to us.

Understanding this first basic truth, that all is in divine order, helps us to reassess all that happens, then look for the greater wisdom the event suggests. If somehow, not always readily apparent, all our experiences and events fit together in some way, we can live proactively and responsibly, not reactively and victimized. Search for the meaning behind the seeming coincidences in your life. Start to see how they are here to bless you and help you to enter and follow the path of joy. Every experience is there to bless you and to serve you. Use this principle to take charge of your life. Most of all, have fun with the "accidental" occurrences in your life for they really are serendipitous opportunities for you.

CHAPTER THREE

PAINFUL REALITIES

As eluded to in the previous chapter, life is not always good news. Sometimes it is made up of the bad news as well. One of the fair things in life is all of us deal with painful realities at one point or another in time. No one seems to be immune from this, regardless of social status, economic status or heritage.

Part of adventurous living is facing and dealing with the painful realities of life. Understanding these occur in our lives, the adventurous approach allows us to transform these painful events into joy over time. While no one likes to have painful realities in their life, these can and must be faced. As they are dealt with, rather than avoided or ignored, then the path of joy can be followed.

Painful realities help us to heal our lives as we face the challenges they present. Transformation at all levels develops by meeting the challenges, facilitating learning and growth. All the while the pain of the adversity of challenge can't be ignored or avoided. Too often we try to anesthetize or completely avoid pain and hurt, but in doing so we create other problems far worse than the pain we are trying to avoid. If we use alcohol or drugs to reduce or avoid pain, we may in the long run create an addiction problem for ourselves far worse than the original pain. The initial pain of abstinence may also end up being far worse than the original hurt or suffering we experienced. In the end, when abstinence is established and the path of recovery is undertaken, the original hurt and pain remain to be healed anyway.

Painful realities unfortunately come in many forms. We are all too familiar with the many ways life can be painful. They are the death of a loved one, a friend, or even a pet. They are an accident that causes injury or pain, or an illness leaving us debilitated for a short time, or perhaps longer or permanently. Illnesses or injuries putting us on disability, unable to function in job roles or a career we worked hard to attain, are painful realities we face.

Painful realities arise with a loved one who is unable to care for themselves, partially or completely. They are an elderly parent who no longer recognizes us or requires nursing home care. It is a loved one who is developmentally disabled, or who suffers from a mental illness they are unable to easily or ever overcome.

Painful realities are the momentary or more significant setbacks occurring in life. They are the loss of a job, or a financial crisis or failure. They are the loss of a relationship, the failure of a marriage, a child who is alienated from her family, or a relative who no longer cares to associate with us. They are the large and small failures we experience throughout the course of a lifetime, whether at home, in our relationships, at work or in our neighborhoods and communities.

Painful realities are disasters or natural calamities. They are sudden changes in our environment, some of which can cause injury or be life-threatening. They are accidents or tragedies directly impacting on us, or tragic events occurring to others we can empathize with or feel a connection with, even when the event happens so very far away.

Painful realities are situations or events causing us to question our belief in an orderly and just universe. They are events leading us to question our fundamental beliefs about many things, including our belief in a Higher Power or Creator.

Painful realities are the moments when the underlying truth about a situation, a relationship, or the condition of our world suddenly punctuates our perception of what we believed to be there before. These can be defining moments helping us to be more aware, replacing the self-delusion we can so easily create for ourselves with our egos.

Most of us like to think of ourselves in the most positive way, especially when we operate solely from our ego. However, there are also some of us who like to think the worst about ourselves and see ourselves as totally unworthy of any good in our lives. Both choices can outwardly manifest in negative and destructive ways, and often we are blind to these less than positive outcomes. For ourselves, it preserves a sense of integrity and tenuous self-worth defined by a limited ego-oriented perception of ourselves and the world.

Even as we grow spiritually, painful reminders occur. Not only are we not any less immune to these painful events, we may actually face more, for as we grow we get more challenges including the painful and difficult ones. The paradox is growth leads to more challenges. Yet shrinking away from growth and all the opportunities, good and bad, that goes with growth only leads to living lives of quiet desperation. Even with painful realities, facing them takes us beyond the ordinary to living extraordinary lives.

Adventurous living is handling these painful realities with grace and calmness, as well as letting these moments aid us in the transformational process so that genuine growth and awareness result. Sudden awareness of how we are perceived by others, or how they "really" think of us, helps us to change behaviors and attitudes which are limiting and self-defeating. Sudden awareness may also help us to move beyond any previous limitations we have put on ourselves, or we have allowed others to put on us. Sometimes sudden awareness helps us to understand our relationships with others, and whether the relationships may need to be re-defined with the new information now available.

One painful reality for me was discovering family members I love and care about did not feel the same, based solely on outward appearances and not who I am. I returned home one year from the annual Christmas family gathering, which we rotate annually between my wife's family. This year was spent in the Philadelphia area, where my sister-in-law and her family reside. My wife and son stayed on an additional week, beyond the time I was able to stay.

Upon returning home, my wife was upset about many unpleasant situations which arose. One situation was an after dinner conversation she was particularly offended by. Several relatives spoke about their dislike of overweight people, in disparaging and derogatory ways. They even questioned how anyone could possibly love a person who is fat, and assured one another that they could not do this.

Besides the overall feeling of prejudice toward overweight people in general, my wife and I also wondered how they must really feel about me, and about her for loving me. Since I have a weight problem, and was significantly overweight until recently, no doubt they must think I am unlovable. While at the time I weighed thirty pounds less than my all-time high, I have many more pounds to lose. By their standards, I was not worthy of love, never mind whatever other qualities I might possess.

While I have always sensed distance and coolness from some of these relatives, it was still a shock to hear how they felt. Although not specifically named, I know I was included in their evaluation of, and attitude toward, people with weight problems. The realization of how they thought was a painful reality for me. Naturally I felt considerable hurt and pain, even more so because I tried to be loving and caring with them.

To say I was stunned would not begin to explain the shock I experienced as this painful reality came crashing into the illusion of hope I carried about our relationships improving with time. I believed at least some caring existed between us, and at some level no doubt it does. However, I am also now painfully aware just how conditional their love is.

I tend to be very hopeful and optimistic with others, often overlooking signs suggesting otherwise. I often try to believe the best about others, and so it frequently comes as a surprise when others feel negatively toward me for whatever reason. Yet I also recognize I am not here to please others or that everyone is going to like me.

All of us have moments when we become unexpectedly aware how others really think or feel about is, often at odds with our own perception of ourselves, or how we think others perceive or feel about us. Since there are no coincidences, this experience with my relatives and the sudden realization of how they felt came into my life for a reason. Partly, I concluded, I simply needed to know I must move on, not expending any more effort or energy in relationships not going anywhere. I still send them my love and extend forgiveness to them, but I have also lowered my expectations of what may come from them.

Next, I realized not everyone is going to appreciate me for who I am spiritually, mentally, emotionally and physically, nor take the time and effort to know me as a person. Even within my own family many may not want to know who I am, what I believe in or what I am about, but would rather focus on the superficial, such as appearance. Even when there are profound differences in belief or philosophy, love and acceptance do not have to be conditional. Each of us is entitled to our own beliefs and ways of living life.

While I would like relatives to be fellow companions in the journey of life, I now know this may not always be possible. The challenge is to accept this reality, accept where they are, accept how limited they are with me, and face all this without rejection, aloofness, bitterness or rancor. The challenge, and the adventure, is to extend love and forgiveness, while accepting the painful truth of these relationships.

All of us are confronted with painful realities, large and small, significant or seemingly insignificant. Since acceptance and approval are important for us, painful realities can puncture our world view and challenge our sense of who we are and how we would like the world to perceive and treat us.

A small event illustrating this happened at a hospital I consulted with. I practice sending friendliness and love to others as I walk around, whether at the hospital, in a store, at the mall or in the neighborhood. I like to smile and greet people, and this is often reciprocated spreading good cheer. If you want friends, be friendly, and if you want happiness, be happy. If you want the world to be a better place, send out positive thought, feeling and light to others and to the world. Projecting white light into the world, surrounding others and the world in a white light, brings greater peace and serenity to the collective world we live in.

If you don't believe this, remember how the opposite effects you. Recall how easily a hateful glare or rude gesture can set off angry, vengeful feelings in you. On the larger scale, the often negative messages and images of our mass media and popular culture can, and do, contribute to pervasive feelings of hopelessness, and a collective belief the world is beyond hope, or only materialism can create happiness.

One day at the hospital I held open the door for a man pushing his pregnant wife in a wheelchair. Suddenly, as he passed me, he leaned toward me and sneered in my face, hissing ominously as we passed by. I was rather startled, especially since I was engaging in an act of kindness, and did not expect this sudden, inexplicable, rude behavior directed toward me.

Why did this man suddenly act like this toward me? Any number of possibilities may have been occurring. Perhaps he just received distressing news about the pregnancy or the health of the baby. Maybe they had just been fighting. Maybe he was frustrated because he had just lost his job, or didn't want the baby in the first place. Maybe it wasn't even his kid. Maybe I was in the wrong place at the wrong time.

It may have been the result of racial differences further compounded by religious identification. An African-American gentleman, he was clothed in Muslim attire. Maybe I was just another "white devil" to be loathed only for the color of my skin.

Whatever the reason, to suddenly be treated in a rude manner for no apparent reason at all regardless of who I am as a person, what I believe, and how I act toward others became a painful reality in that moment. How often do we create painful realities for others, whether we feel justified in our reason or just because we are dumping our pain and anger elsewhere?

How often do we mistreat others based on judgmental and prejudiced views? How often do we ourselves condemn others for the differences which exist amongst us, whether racial, ethnic, religious, cultural, gender, geographical or due to sexual orientation? How painful is the reality when we recognize others are doing the same to us? Yet, these moments can also help us to see ourselves honestly, to know we can't always have others see us for who we truly are, and to give us the ongoing challenges that facilitate our own learning and growth.

One of the reasons we are on this planet is to learn how to accept and appreciate differences, and not condemn those who are not like us. God created a wonderful and rich fabric with humankind. How presumptuous of us to decide only certain ones amongst us are worthy, and all others are simply to be discarded or judged unworthy.

What are we going to do when we realize the fabric of all God's creation is much richer in weave than we can now imagine? How are we going to react when we begin meeting the many different beings existing on other planets and in other star systems? For we are going to be meeting them very soon, within the next few decades if not within the next few years. How narrow and parochial will our judgements and condemnations seem then?

Painful realities sometimes come when we strive for success, but end up experiencing failure instead. This happened to me after I was promoted to be the director for the Michigan operation of a nationwide managed care company. Prior to my promotion my still, small voice within warned me, "be careful what you ask for, for you just might get it." Even with the warning, I celebrated the promotion I had been visualizing and affirming for myself.

Initially I was successful in the new position, but it wasn't long before success turned into numerous challenges and disasters difficult to manage one by one let alone all at once. The worst problems included a lawsuit alleging malpractice, ongoing tension with the local psychiatric community about managed care new to the local area, pressure to see clients while understaffed for the need, and a supervisor who seemed more interested in "mind games" at times than in providing leadership and positive supervision and support.

The role was also a middle-level management position where I was often caught in a no win position between upper-level managers who thought I was not doing enough to run the operation profitably, and lower level supervisors and staff who thought I had lost touch with them and did not hear their concerns. Some staff even thought I had "sold out" to the company. So much for being careful what I had asked for, for I really was getting more than I bargained for.

Within a year it was increasingly clear I was no longer viewed as a promising new manager, and was instead viewed as a probable liability. Not that this ever addressed with me directly. Instead the latter emerged in increasingly distant behavior by my immediate supervisor, as well as unkind behavior and at times blatantly rude behavior by corporate managers.

One telling occasion was at a regional quarterly meeting. I was treated with cool contempt and borderline rude behavior. On the elevator one time I was completely ignored as though I did not exist. Thus, it came as no surprise the following month when I was demoted, although I was still expected to fulfill the same responsibilities as before. At least my still, small voice reassured me as I drove to the airport prior to the meeting in Indianapolis when I was to be demoted. The still, small voice within simply stated, "It is not your time yet, your time will come."

Another painful reality involved one of my supervisors, who had also been in contention with me for the director position. She was undermining my relationship with staff members and sabotaging how I wanted the operation to run. She manipulated secretaries to sabotage the work of the administration assistant who reported directly to me.

Unbeknownst to me at the time, she was also going behind my back, calling my supervisor to complain about how I was running things and stating I was the reason morale was so poor.

A meeting was "staged" at one point purportedly to allow the staff to voice their concerns with my manager. Many half-truths, distortions and outright lies were shared without me or the subordinate supervisor present. No matter how secret organizations try to be, however, the truth always emerges in the end. Many staff approached me after the meeting to let me know what was going on. My supervisor seized the opportunity to emotionally berate me for my seeming failure, acting out his own mean streak while I was in a vulnerable position and not yet fully aware of the truth of what actually took place in this staged meeting.

While I no doubt made many of my own mistakes along the way, and sometimes acted in less than the highest ethical sense as defined by universal laws, the actions toward me by senior management and by staff below were inexcusable. Nevertheless, I have to accept full responsibility for my part in the failure I experienced.

This episode in my life was truly a challenging adventure, one that called upon me to further learn and practice the virtues of patience, long-suffering, calmness and forgiveness. It took considerable effort and time to heal the hurt and resentment I felt at the way I was treated.

Unfortunately, other painful adventures were only beginning at this time in my life. While I already was seeking alternative employment, the contract between the health maintenance organization and the managed mental health care company I worked for was canceled, half-way through a four year contract. Although I was already developing options for myself, the prospect of being without a major source of income was frightening. To make matters worse, we purchased our new home shortly before this happened. With this was a sizable increase in our mortgage payment, as well as the depletion of our savings.

One low moment was putting my son to bed one night as he tearfully shared his fear we would lose our house. In anger I imaged the pain I wanted to inflict on the medical director of the health company and his cohorts, as well as the management of the health care company I worked for, for the pain they caused my family and myself. Often when we hurt we want to hurt others, but this isn't the way to face a painful reality!

The replacement company was not willing to hire me in spite of my good reputation and excellent clinical skills. The nemesis supervisor, who sabotaged the previous operation, was hired as their new clinic director. She gave them an ultimatum she would quit if they hired me, which they clearly wanted to do initially.

Philosophically, I intuitively knew God wanted me elsewhere, but it remained frustrating and painful to have an uncertain future. Thankfully, new opportunities came along as needed, albeit slowly. These opportunities came serendipitously, and opened doors that have subsequently led to much greater abundance, prosperity and success than I could hardly imagine at the time.

These opportunities also led to discoveries in treatment I have begun to use with great success as traditional modes of psychological treatment have been enhanced by emerging metaphysical forms of treatment.

Finances were extremely tight initially as the previous job came to an end. Fortunately, vacation and sick time helped to carry me over for a while. However, the company did not honor its severance pay policy, making finances more strained than they needed to be at first. Even with this, we had enough coming in to cover expenses and pay taxes all but one month.

While new opportunities arose and gradually began to pay off, we went through a 25% reduction in income, after having taken on more than double the house payment and after having depleted all savings. Further, I now had to buy my own health insurance, as well as pay additional social security taxes due to being self-employed. By February there was just enough income to cover expenses for the month, with nothing left over for taxes.

During the subsequent time period some job opportunities I was well qualified for, and which would have eased our burden, would not open for me. Before Christmas, a director position I hoped for went to someone else. Certainly I was going through a very serious and challenging period in my life, one which would later provide me with greater strength and endurance. It tested, yet developed, my faith and challenged me to grow spiritually. It was a very painful reality but one which, in retrospect, gave me many gifts and propelled me forward on my own path of joy.

The lowest I felt was during the following February. On top of financial stress and professional disappointment, I also became ill with first, the gout, and then, the flu. The gout is a crystal arthritic condition which attacks joints. Interestingly, according to Louise Hay, it also represents anger and impatience. I was experiencing plenty of anger, frustration and impatience as I wanted my life in order and at ease immediately. The gout literally forced me to slow down and become more patient. Even the painful realities of sickness and poor health afford great opportunities to learn lessons and move forward.

I learned I had to let go, release my anger and frustration, and practice the spiritual principles I believed to be true. I had to do this while feeling so low that when the flu came along, I lay on the couch and quietly cried, the painful reality of life was so intense at that time.

I could have tried to avoid the painful reality, deny the pain, and not acknowledge to myself and others what a difficult time I was having. I could have easily blamed others, become self-righteous and angry with everyone. I could have felt entitled to different outcomes, and rejected God for having to go through a painful reality. During painful realities we do experience these and other reactions. In facing the painful reality and coping with all the negative and fear-based emotions that go with it, true joy and happiness eventually emerge.

Painful realities can take us by surprise at times. Consulting at an inpatient residential treatment addictions program for a many years I believed I was accepted enough by the staff that I felt comfortable soliciting for my son's school fund-raiser. Having sold at other facilities I was quite taken aback by the response I received. The reaction was tantamount to how dare I bring this fund-raiser to them. It was conveyed in comments and assumptions of my being wealthy and not needing to support my son's fund-raiser, the school not needing the funds because it was in a better school district, and that I and other parents in the area I live in could easily get what was needed without a fund-raiser.

One nurse I thought of as a friend, was particularly virulent in her comments and attitude. She took offense I would ask her to participate in a fund-raising activity for a "rich" school. I was stunned and then embarrassed. It was a painful reality, for the sudden realization of how they felt created considerable embarrassment for me.

Painful realities can surprise us, and continuously remind us, of the consequences of judgmental behavior humankind engages in all to readily. Beyond that, they become opportunities for adventurous living. For life is filled with moments of pain and suffering. We all have to face challenges which are accompanied by hurt and pain. What we do with these painful realities shapes the rest of our lives and ultimately creates joy. There is no shortcut through them; we must face and meet these challenges. As we do so we learn and grow, and the stumbling blocks become stepping stones to our greater good.

Painful realities, whether brought on by ourselves, or part of our "curriculum" for this lifetime, are part of our great adventure. Milly Collins, a Unity minister, shares the story of a rape victim who was interviewed on a television talk show. She was viciously assaulted, a painful reality that took weeks for her to recover from. She was questioned about her amazing ability to get on with her life in a productive, successful way without bitterness about what had happened to her in the past. She answered, "The rapist forcibly stole one day of my life. Bringing that day back is out of my control. But there is no way I'm going to willingly give him control over all of my tomorrows and let him victimize me the rest of my life by reliving the incident." Not only has this person accepted the wisdom of not living in the past, she has transformed a painful reality with her attitude.

We are not to suppress, reject or hate painful realities. It is alright, however, not to like them whether we are currently experiencing one or just knowing one will come along in due time. It is important to recognize them as part of the challenge of life. They are not easy to deal with or to live through. They can and will come into our lives again and again. Yet it is these most difficult moments of pain and adversity which offer us the most growth, development, wisdom and awareness.

Make the most of all situations, even the painful moments of life. Do not shirk from their challenge, or create even more challenging painful realities through avoidance behavior. Remember, even when the hour seems darkest, and you feel you can't go on another minute, the moment you decide to face the painful event with courage and the desire to benefit from it, the painful reality will transform you. It will truly become a stepping stone to your greater good.

CHAPTER FOUR

LIFE'S LESSONS

Since there are no coincidences, and everything including painful realities are happening for a reason, adventurous living is about discovering what the lesson or lessons are in each situation. By accepting the lessons life has to offer, specifically and generally, greater wisdom develops. As we understand the lessons of life we gain an increased awareness of how basic truths operate, always for our greater good. Everything that happens allows us to learn and grow physically, mentally, emotionally and spiritually.

Increased physical health and atunement does result when we learn from life's lessons. At the most basic level within our cellular structure, increased harmony physically arises when life is managed and when the lessons are received. Meeting the challenges and lessons of life also lead to greater harmony in our emotional lives, allowing ourselves to become more attuned mentally and achieving self-actualization. Finally, life's lessons allow for greater spiritual attainment.

The planet we live on is a classroom, a special place of learning in this universe. In part it is special because as spiritual beings we come here to learn about the physical dimensions. We do this so we can understand third dimensional reality first, then evolve into greater dimensional awareness and understanding beyond the fundamental physical dimensions, for fourth, fifth and sixth dimensional realities are more fluid but have some physicality to them.

We come to learn about physicality at the slowest and heaviest vibrational level, and the universal laws associated with physicality, such as cause and effect. More importantly, within this classroom we again discover our true spiritual heritage after the veil of forgetfulness is drawn over us at the time of our birth. We learn how spirit operates within the context of physical form, whether third, fourth or fifth dimensional awareness.

This is by no means not the only classroom in the universe, for there are worlds without number. Yet contained within this classroom are the unique lessons associated with this particular planet. The souls created for this planet, or those created for other planets who come to reside here, get to experience the unique lessons and opportunities this place has to offer.

Everything is an opportunity to learn. Even seeming failure and adversity contain within them the seeds of greater understanding, clarity and vision. Within each lifetime there are many chances to experience all facets of life, to gain in appreciation and understanding, and to fulfill the unique potential contained within each of us.

Life continuously presents challenges. Oftentimes we try to avoid the challenges, to look for easier ways out, to find ways to deal with situations as they present themselves. This becomes especially true when the challenge is adversity. Yet life will continually present us with the same challenge or situation over and over again, until they are faced and dealt with. It is in facing the challenges that true happiness and joy result. All attempts to avoid challenges lead to depression, anxiety, dissatisfaction or boredom. Lives that are ordinary or worse yet lives of quiet desperation result when we don't meet challenges.

Each situation offers a lesson, a chance to learn something to better understand ourself or to understand another, to learn a new skill or to develop a new ability. Each situation or event also provides a chance to learn patience, to express and receive love, and to make the world a better place with a positive attitude or response. While we may not be able to change the world by ourself, we can make our corner of the world a better place to be. However, don't underestimate your ability to change the whole world, for every change begins with an idea someone has.

One of the primary lessons on this planet is to give and to receive love. Not just the intimate, romantic kind existing between two lovers, but a deeper, greater, abiding love which can be expressed to all others and all creation. Even intimate, romantic love develops into a deeper, abiding, mutual love which grows between two people as they face the ongoing challenges in their relationship over time. For when two people live together, face challenges together, fight and argue together and work together to meet their challenges and resolve their conflicts, this deep, abiding love does grow, a love which transcends the initial infatuation that brought them together. Ultimately, complete and unconditional love emerges.

The development of unconditional love is one of the general life lessons learned in this classroom. Unconditional means love expressed without any reservations, without statements one will only be loved or lovable if certain conditions are met. Statements to oneself or another that "I will only love you if you do this or do that requirement" become conditional.

This is not to be confused with "tough love" which says "I love you, but I will no longer accept dysfunctional behavior." The latter says the person makes a choice to no longer participate in a dysfunctional relationship, but does not withhold love. The most loving thing a person can say to an alcoholic is "I love you, but I will no longer live with you if you continue to drink." They are not rejecting the person, but taking care of themselves. Hopefully, they also reach the other person, helping them to recognize the consequences of their behavior and the negative effects their behavior has produced in the relationship.

The truth about tough love is the person is saying "I love you enough to no longer participate in this destructive path with you." There is an asking for change, but not a withholding of love. There is discernment which says the negative behavior is not condoned, and which may further say I will no longer be with you if you persist in this destructive path. The limit is set with love and care, but the boundary has to be established, especially since your own well-being is equally important. You do have the right and obligation to yourself to take good care of you first.

Taking good care of ourselves is the first and foremost love. Self-love is learning to love ourselves and express self-love. Self-worth is key to developing the capacity to be love and to express love to others. To be love is ultimately to express the same love God continuously gives to us, loving ourselves and accepting ourselves unconditionally.

Yet so often we find this is difficult to do. Go look in a mirror, look directly at yourself making eye contact, and tell yourself, "I love you." Does the very thought of doing this make you uncomfortable? Go do this anyway. What happened? How difficult was it for you to look yourself in the eye and say these words? Were you able to do it completely, or only partly? How much did you hesitate before you were able to tell yourself you care about you? Did you feel awkward, anxious, silly or selfish? How so very difficult it can be to love ourselves!

Yet each of us is an individualized expression of God. Each of us is and continues to be worthy in God's mind. Each of us is God in action at our point in the universe. How can we consider ourselves less than what God considers us? What possible guilt, blame or shame can we put on ourselves when God already sees us as worthy, and has already forgiven us? Isn't it supreme arrogance to say to ourselves it is well and good God loves us completely and unconditionally, but I will still withhold love to myself? Learning to be and express self-love and self-worth is an important life lesson. The song, "The Greatest Love of All" sums up this lesson beautifully.

There is a wonderful affirmation from the St. Germain I AM materials which sums up creation of self-love and self-worth. It also creates healing and atunement at all levels. The affirmation is said out loud as you look at yourself in the mirror. It goes something as follows:

> Through the Intelligence and Beauty
> I AM, I command you to take on
> Perfect Beauty of form, for I AM that
> Beauty in every cell of which you are
> composed. You shall respond to my
> command and become radiantly beautiful
> in every way, in thought, word,
> feeling and form. I AM the Fire and
> Beauty of your eyes and I carry forth
> this Radiant Energy into everything
> which I look.

As I shared earlier, I was diagnosed with adult-onset diabetes. The healing taking place for me physically would not be possible without my deciding my worthiness and loving myself totally and completely. This hurdle of adult-onset diabetes becomes an opportunity to truly manifest self-love and self-worth, allowing me to begin the process of healing on all levels and to begin walking the path of joy in my life.

The next aspect of love we learn about on this planet is love of others, including those who are closest to us such as spouses, children, parents and family members. Learning to love others then extends to friends, neighbors and members of our community. Naturally, it often is easier to love those closest to us, but the challenge is to love everyone unconditionally.

Loving others is remembering to look beyond surface behavior to the true spiritual essence within each person. I may not like another's behavior, but this does not make them less worthy of love. I do not have to accept or condone their behavior, and may even choose not to relate to them because of their behavior, yet they are still worthy of love from me. Ultimately this makes it much easier to let go of resentment, anger and judgment. It is learning to behold the Christ in another, their true spiritual heritage.

Love extends to all of humanity, for we truly are all one. Instead of seeing differences, based on the many ways humanity tries to define itself separately, these same differences can instead be honored and celebrated. One of the purposes of this classroom is to know and accept differences, whether we always agree or not, so we can become true Co-Creators with God. We are hear to learn, understand and accept differences. God didn't create all these differences, just so we can claim we are the one exclusive group worthy of His love and acceptance. Universal love, and Love which unconditionally creates and nurtures us, requires extending that same love accepting and celebrating the rich fabric of life as it unfolds in our many differences.

We are here to love, accept and enjoy all of life as it manifests on this planet. Unconditional love also extends to the animal and plant kingdoms. The Native Americans and other indigenous people remind us how to be in touch with the brotherhood of all life at all levels. Even in science basic ecology and biology demonstrate all life works in harmony, each part essential to the whole. Learning to understand, accept and love life in all its forms is part of leaning love, and the ultimate Love which created this universe and everything in it.

Ultimately, we are to love this planet, which nurtures us and gives us life. Increased awareness reveals Mother Earth is a living being with her own consciousness. When we learn to love her and thank her for her nurturance of and sustenance of us, and when we learn to live in harmony with her, we extend back to her the great love she gives us.

Finally, suppose there really are "space," or cosmic, brothers and sisters we are about to meet. Apparently some of us have already met them. Imagine the diversity which must exist in the entire universe, given the diversity on this planet alone. Are we ready to meet, get to know and learn to love "alien" life forms?

A test of this may well come very soon, if we make contact and meet our cosmic brothers and sisters from other planets and constellations. Personally, I find it rather presumptuous to assume in the vastness of a universe in which there are worlds without end, life would only exist on this remote planet circling an obscure star in one galaxy.

The second general lesson offered in this classroom is patience. We are here to learn patience, both with ourselves and with others. Patience is related to judgment, whether directed at ourselves or others. As we judge we express impatience with ourselves and with others about who we are, where we are on life's journey, and whether we are more or less worthy than someone else. Patience ultimately means moving beyond judgment.

Judgment is difficult to let go of, because from the moment we are born we are taught judgment. Partly judgment is learned to help discriminate and perceive difference. Unfortunately, over time we are also taught prejudice and learn to discriminate against others.

Humanity often finds differences threatening, and uses the perception of "out groups" to create more cohesion within one's own group. While some amount of judgment is necessary and useful, when judgment leads to discrimination, prejudice, contempt or condemnation then it no longer serves a useful purpose for anyone. Patience requires accepting differences, and also accepting someone where they are at, not where we would like them to be.

Watching the Discovery Channel recently, I was saddened to see a documentary on the radical Muslim fundamentalists in Egypt. One gentleman made the remark that "all Christians and Jews are not worthy to live." Here was a person who did not know me or you, wasn't aware of our common humanity nor our common spiritual essence within, yet he was willing to judge many unworthy to live. This kind of thinking isn't restricted to the Muslim world, but exists in many ideological and religious groups.

It would be easy to judge back, to condemn this man for his belief. Yet the challenge of this and all similar situations is to practice patience, to understand the forces leading this person to his belief, and hopefully one day make him aware of the greater truths governing this universe. While his hatred grows out of poverty, powerlessness and despair, the opportunity also exists from those same experiences to learn patience and overcome those circumstances by contributing positively to the world.

Anyone who is a parent can truly appreciate the concept of patience. For no matter what our agenda may be for our child, they grow and unfold at their own pace. Patience is required to teach them self-control, without destroying their spirit, their natural sense of adventure within. Patience is remembering they will develop with loving guidance and teaching, combined with firm discipline and limits. Patience is letting them grow, with loving nurturance, at the pace needed for optimal achievement of each developmental milestone.

Patience is particularly required during those challenging ages when their personalities must become disorganized, so they can reintegrate at a higher level of functioning and identity. True patience is required in tolerating all the miserable behavior that goes with these transitions.

My son is thirteen, and has entered one of these transitional ages. Profound patience is often needed as his hormones begin to rage, his mood fluctuates wildly, he becomes extremely sensitive and is emotionally volatile. I tell him at least once a week he won't live to be fourteen. Yet, through it all, I know patience, steadfastness and evenness of response is necessary so he can traverse this developmental period safely, achieve a new level of integration, and continue the adventure of becoming who he is and must be. While I try to be patient with him, I am hardly perfect and end up yelling at him anyway at times.

Patience is allowing a process to unfold as it must with its own time table. The Biblical passage from Ecclesiastics sums this up nicely, "For every time there is a season, for every time there is a reason, under Heaven."

If the course of life is likened to a river, when we are on the river we can only see as far as the next bend. From this limited perspective, life does not make sense at times. Yet if we gradually rise above the river, the higher we rise, the more of the river we can see. Life's twists and turns are like the river, seemingly without course or purpose at times. Yet as we attain higher awareness, we begin to see the twists and turns do make sense, that life does unfold with meaning, purpose and learning.

In the moment an event may make no sense, and is sometimes pure madness, but over time the event emerges as a seminal event needed for our lives to unfold perfectly. Tragedies and seeming setbacks, as well as miraculous events all happen as they should. When dealing with a setback or a delay, remember that greater good is at work as your divine plan unfolds for you. Patience requires acceptance that all is happening as it should.

At times life seems to flow smoothly, and everything appears to fall into place as it should. The more aware we become, and the more we attune to higher spiritual law, the more relationships, prosperity, opportunities and events flow evenly in our lives. Yet even when we practice faith and trust in the universe and with God, there still are plenty of times the divine plan is different than how we want it to be. Patience requires we wait on the greater plan, allowing it to unfold in our life and accepting the course it takes for us at times.

The greatest challenge in the lesson of patience is with others, especially loved ones. In recognizing each person is exactly where they are supposed to be in their journey, patience requires us to let them learn and grow according to their curriculum. While we may offer guidance and feedback to them, it is not up to us to impose our ideas on them of where they should be or how they should go about it.

Too often people are busy trying to tell each other how to live rather than dealing with their own lessons. It sure is a lot easier to tell others what they should be doing, rather than meeting our own challenges and working on our own growth. Many of us would rather tell someone else what to do or how to be, rather than take care of our own challenges.

This process of self-avoidance is so pervasive we have religious leaders and politicians who sincerely believe they know what is best for us, not wanting us to use our own free will to make the best decisions for ourselves. Each one of us faces the challenge to look within ourselves, and to let others do the same for themselves. Patience is the long-suffering and the calm ability to let others have their experiences, their challenges, their choices and their adventures.

Related to patience is the life lesson of judgment. Learning not to judge others is one of the greatest challenges in this classroom. All major religions have taught this great truth. Jesus stated it as "Judge not lest ye be judged." What he was teaching is the truth that as we pass judgment on others, so will the same judgment be passed on to us.

Judgment often implies a sense of superiority, that one is better than another. Whether as an action or a belief, judging someone suggests we are assuming a superior position. Judgment is not to be confused with discernment. Discernment helps me to evaluate and make choices between various options. Part of discernment may be deciding one choice is better than another.

If one is comfortable with their beliefs and actions, that should be sufficient. One does not have to judge another to be all right with their position. When judgment is combined with self-righteousness, the error is compounded. This does not mean one should not develop a high ethical and moral value system, just that in doing so one remembers to retain humility and not condemn anyone else. Even as Jesus chastised the pharisees and hypocrites of his day, he loved them and forgave them.

We can disagree about ideas and have differences of opinion. We can argue for a particular viewpoint. Passing judgment is the error to be avoided. Accepting differences is a life lesson on this planet. Considering the multitude of differences in culture, language, belief, custom and politics, differences are certainly a reality on this planet. Yet we often become provincial, assuming our way of doing things is the only way, and the right way as well.

Instead of learning from others, we close ourselves off to learning from others and experiencing new things. Enjoy, appreciate and honor your heritage, but also learn to enjoy, appreciate and honor other heritages as well. Part of increased awareness is awareness of how others live, love, find joy and find God.

We are on this planet to learn about good and evil. We don't have to experience evil to learn about it, all we have to do is look around at all the consequences of evil in the world about us. Evil is not just the obvious wrongdoing we perceive, but also the more subtle wrongdoing which creates havoc and harm. An unkind word, a harsh judgment, a seemingly minor violation of right action are all part of evil. Edgar Cayce, noted American prophet, once said in a trance reading, "each day we face a choice between good and evil, choose good."

A religious secretary at one of the hospitals I consult at shared with a co-worker the church I attend is a cult, a place which does not believe in Jesus Christ, and where only pagans attend. Ironically, the person she shared this with happens to be Jewish. The church I attend simply has a different concept of who Jesus was and the meaning of the messages he brought to the world. While my church has one understanding of the truth he taught, I know her church also provides another understanding of that truth. I may not agree with all her church teaches but I respect that it is the best place for her to achieve her spiritual growth and development. If I differ with you, choosing good means I can accept your choice even when we disagree.

There are many lessons about good and evil in life. They are available daily, not only in the news but also immediately in our lives. They can be as great as criminal behavior, or as minor as unkind words, small lies or self-justified dishonesty. We continually face choices about good and evil.

The Ten Commandments remain the best guide on making these choices. Ten simple, but profound, rules of conduct are contained in these commandments. They refer not just to behavior, but also to how we think and feel. It certainly becomes much more complicated when thought and feeling are included. However, even war begins with the anger, hatred and malice harbored within each individual. Murderous thoughts are as destructive as murder itself, for eventually it manifests in the latter at a societal level. Choosing between good and evil includes all we think, feel and do.

Another life lesson is learning how to love God while we are in the physical. In the physical our consciousness becomes limited, particularly as we rely upon our senses rather than our true spiritual nature within. Yet even in the physical we are surrounded by the beauty of God's creation. Such wonderful detail surrounds us, even on this minor and seemingly insignificant planet, in one galaxy, in one universe.

As we again begin to appreciate and marvel at the physical realm, we begin to experience love of God. The soothing effect of the beauty which surrounds us reminds us of the peace that passes all understanding. It is the recognition of our love of God and our unity with God. Jesus taught we are to love God, and then love others as we love God. He stated that all the commandments and all the law rested on these two spiritual truths.

Finally, the greatest life lesson we learn on this planet is how to become Co-Creators with God. To do this we journey through time and space and come to this planet to learn all of the lessons offered here. We are then able to return to be Co-Creators with Him/Her. For God is constantly expanding creation. Who is to say that some day each one of us won't be responsible for creation in a new universe, planet or place. To prepare for this we go through many experiences so we can freely choose to return to God with complete awareness. From there we can truly become Co-Creators.

We learn about creation on this planet as we choose, and as our lives unfold based on our beliefs and choices. Napoleon Hill once wrote, "what the mind can conceive, and believe, it can achieve." Mind is the builder. Thoughts and beliefs create our reality. If you don't like how your life is right now, change how you believe, and change your thoughts about what you want to experience.

I use two simple, but powerful, affirmations with clients with incredible results. For relationships I instruct them to say, "The perfect relationship is coming to me now." I have them say this command out loud ten times each night before they go to bed. If my client needs a new job I have them say, "The perfect job is coming to me now." When stated with conviction incredible results emerge in people's lives. Begin to create a new reality. Change your mind and you change your life.

Life offers us many lessons. Greet each day with the expectation that the lessons are there, waiting to be learned. As life's lessons are learned, spiritual truth emerges. Adventurous living is eagerly meeting these lessons, as well as our particular lessons, day by day.

Whether the personal lessons or the general lessons we need arise, the following "rules of being human" best summarize the process on this planet. These rules are as follows:

The Rules For Being Human

1. **You will receive a body.** You may like it or hate it, but it will be yours for the entire period this time around.
2. **You will learn lessons.** You are enrolled in a full time, informal school called "life." Each day in this school you have the opportunity to learn lessons. You may like the lessons or think them irrelevant and stupid.
3. **There are no mistakes, only lessons.** Growth is a process of trial and error, experimentation. The "failed" experiments are as much a part of the process as the experiment that ultimately "works."
4. **A lesson is repeated until it is learned.** A lesson will be presented to you in various forms until you have learned it. Then you

can go on to the next lessons.

5. **Learning lessons does not end.** There is no part of life that does not contain its lessons. If you are alive, there are lessons to be learned.

6. **"There" is no better than "here."** When your "there" has become a "here," you will simply obtain another "there" that again, looks better than "here."

7. **Others are merely mirrors of you.** You cannot love or hate something about another person unless it reflects to you something you love or hate about yourself.

8. **What you make of your life is up to you.** You have all the tools and resources you'll need; what you do with them is up to you. The choice is yours.

9. **The answers lie inside you.** The answers to life's questions lie inside you. All you need to do is look, listen, and trust.

Understanding life is about lessons, the adventurous approach lets us recognize they are available to us on an ongoing basis. Understanding the lessons we meet life daily, we can apply them to create joy in our lives. Enjoy this classroom, and make the most of it, responsibly putting into action what you learn day by day.

CHAPTER FIVE

MY DELUSIONS, OR
HOW I THINK THE UNIVERSE WORKS

Having presented some basic truths that there are no coincidences, that life is filled with painful realities at times, and that there are lessons we are here to learn, other universal truths operate which are helpful to be aware of to enter and follow the path of joy. Understanding how these basic truths operate assists us in creating our lives as masterpieces of joy.

In my own studies of a wide variety of subjects, over the years, and watching the serendipitous events unfolding in my life, I have drawn some conclusions about how this universe operates. I present these as my delusion, for I have no proof to offer you these truths and principles exist. I have just come "to know" certain principles and truths. What I am presenting is by no means conclusive or inclusive.

As awareness and understanding expand, greater wisdom seems to emerge for all. Whether the wisdom obtained by others or the wisdom which I have obtained, I have come to accept some of these ideas as truth. However, each person is free to draw their own conclusions as their awareness expands and grows for them.

First and foremost, I accept that we live in a lawful universe. Just as science has concluded certain laws exist within the physical universe, allowing physical matter to be held together in particular, predictable ways, so too, universal laws exist at the metaphysical level. Many of the religious traditions of the world define and indicate how these universal truths operate.

As we evaluate our lives and the way events unfold, we too can observe how these laws operate through our experiences. Although life may seem random and accidental, the underlying reality is a lawful universe operates continuously. We may not always be aware of how events respond to lawful parameters, but they do so nonetheless.

The first law was taught by the master teacher Jesus as "What you sow, so shall you reap." All religious traditions and master teachers have taught a variation of this. The basic principle is what we do returns to us. If we put out hate and fear, the same will be returned to us. If we put out love, justice, mercy or kindness, the same will also be returned to us.

A related principle of this law has been referred to as the law of tenfold return, because not only do things return to us, but they return ten times over. This is the foundation behind tithing 10% of one's income, for it insures a continued flow of good and prosperity in our life. If I put out unkindness into the universe, either ten times the unkindness or ten different acts of unkindness will come back to me. If I put out positive- and love-based emotions and actions they will also return to me tenfold, either with ten times the intensity or by ten different expressions.

This is the basic law of cause and effect, for one truly does create their life and their reality by what they do. However, this law extends beyond action, and includes our thoughts. How we think about another person or situation also creates our reality. If we harbor resentment or jealousy, this too will be experienced toward ourselves at some point in time. On the other hand, if we are charitable and forgiving the same will also return to us.

Another complication to be aware of is although the results or consequences, both positive and negative, of our thoughts and actions can immediately manifest, this does not necessarily occur all the time. We may not reap what we sow for months or years to come, or even until another lifetime or in another dimensional awareness.

However, "God is not mocked," which means that in a lawful universe "what goes around" does indeed "come around." A dramatic way I experienced this was in the following way. Right before I graduated from high school I was fired from a pharmacy I worked at. While intoxicated on graduation night my friends and I decided to seek revenge on the pharmacy, which we accomplished by trashing their delivery car. Regrettably, we did considerable damage to the vehicle.

While I did not initiate this, I did go along. I could use being drunk as an excuse, but I am accountable for my choices, thoughts and actions. About 12 years later I owned a luxury car, and was hit by a hit-and-run driver, doing considerable damage to the back end of my vehicle. I didn't even get upset, for I "knew" in an instant this law was operating in my life, and what I did at an earlier age was returned to me.

The full implication of this law is we are fully and completely accountable for our life. We have total responsibility. Since there are no coincidences, as this law operates we truly reap what we sow. Even if an event is not a consequences for a past thought or deed, it is there as a lesson we are meant to learn. We are responsible to learn the lesson. One can try to blame and externalize responsibility but in the end no one is responsible for our life except ourselves.

The other implication of this law is one doesn't have to seek revenge or "pay back" anyone who has hurt or harmed them. Since each person's actions and thoughts do return to them, one does not have to be the instrument to exact retribution. This is what is meant by "vengeance is mine sayeth the Lord." God is not a harsh, judgmental, vindictive, nor fearsome Creator. However, he has set up a lawful universe so we do experience the results of our actions and thoughts.

Another name for this principle is the law of karma, the concept behind the law of tenfold return, especially as it operates for humanity on this planet. Oftentimes, our conception of karma is limited to negative results, but karma itself is neutral. We experience the results of our thoughts and actions, both positive and negative. If we created hate, we will experience hate to understand how it felt to be the recipient of hate. If we abused a child, we may experience a childhood in which we are the abused to learn the hurt and pain we caused for another.

I attended a past life recall session, during which the psychic would recall a relevant lifetime for each group participant. A woman was told she was a telegraph operator in the American West during her previous lifetime. As a man in that life, she hated the Native Americans, doing everything she could to heap abuse and mistreatment upon them. One result of the karmic debt she created for herself was being killed by an arrow during a raid on the town. Her anger and hate returned to her in the violence in which that lifetime ended. Not surprisingly, in this lifetime she is a minority, learning further lessons about the consequences of discrimination and prejudice.

At one time in my life I was informed by the psychic, Alexia, that seemingly random rudeness I was experiencing from strangers was karmic debt by souls I mistreated in other lifetimes. It helped me to handle the irritations and seeming injustices more calmly.

This does not mean all events in our lives are karmic in nature. Events happen for other reasons, or perhaps for no apparent reason at all. How we respond to the events in life determines future outcomes, either the creation of karmic blessings or debt.

The implication of this law should be increasingly clear. The ongoing reality we create for ourselves is based on what we do and how we think. If my thoughts and actions create my future, then it behooves me to employ actions and thoughts which will bring the best results for me in the future. Disharmony and disorder can disappear from future "time lines" by what is created now. Each of us must begin to think and act more clearly, understanding what we put out does indeed return. Think how differently your life can be if you think and act understanding these truths and how they operate. Think what the world will become when everyone thinks and acts knowing their actions and thoughts will indeed return to them. You really can change your future!

This should especially help us when responding to adversity, for in understanding these principles, we can truly choose to let go of anger and resentment with love and forgiveness, creating a better future for ourselves.

These principles help us to remember what goes around will come around to the person perpetuating the adversity or injustice, and thus one does not have to be vengeful and be the instrument to punish the person for what they did to us. Let someone else or something else resolve the karmic debt.

Create for yourself karmic abundance and good by choosing the higher path. Let universal justice handle the negative and harmful things people do to one another. This does not preclude society from protecting itself from those who can't abide by the rules we all agree to live by. However, in the administration of those rules I do not have to be vindictive or vengeful, otherwise I set in motion karmic consequences for myself I really don't want returning to me later on.

The good news about negative experiences in our lives is another universal law exists which supersedes the law of karma. This is called the law of grace. The law of grace allows us to move beyond the law of karma, especially with regard to the negative consequences of past thought and action, while also enhancing the positive outcomes of karma. The law of grace is simply that we forgive others and love others unconditionally, we cancel out karmic debt for ourselves, heal others and heal the collective consciousness of humanity. By practicing love, forgiveness, charity, compassion, patience and long-suffering with others, we are able to move beyond and to reverse negative karmic debt. This is one major reason why at any time we can truly transform our lives.

As we practice the law of grace it is helpful to begin with the recognition the other person did the best they could, with what they knew, at the time. I might not care very much about their choices, but I begin to accept how the other person's limited awareness led to the behavior which caused pain, hurt or harm to another.

The law of grace essentially reminds us not to judge others, whether through condemnation or vengeance. This doesn't mean we shouldn't imprison the child molester or the murderer, for the protection of everyone is important, and some people lose the right to live with everyone else in freedom. However, we shouldn't harbor condemnation or judgment of the person as well. Jesus unconditionally taught we should not judge, lest we be judged accordingly.

Judgment interferes with our ability to manifest the law of grace in our lives. Ultimately, judgment interferes with the adventure of knowing others. Judgment stems from fear, the basic emotion opposite of love. Jesus taught and demonstrated by his life and actions we are to forgive completely and unconditionally. He did not make any exceptions, nor did he expect us to make exceptions.

This means we can't say I will forgive everyone but the one

individual or group I find most horrible, offensive or unlovable. Even a Hitler, a Saddam Hussein, a child molester or a brutal, serial killer is worthy of forgiveness. As we extend forgiveness to all, we learn to be charitable and loving, and we employ the law of grace in life.

When we forgive others, we forgive ourselves for our own errors in thought and action, and for the deeply hidden part of ourselves that is capable of doing the same things we find unacceptable in others. Who has not harbored a murderous thought in their life time? Elizabeth Kubler-Ross once said in order to know our goodness we had to accept our darkness. She stated, "To know your Mother Theresa, you have to accept your Hitler." Forgiveness is ultimately about ourself.

As we forgive and don't judge, the law of grace manifests in unconditional love for all. I do not have to like another's actions or thoughts, but I can see beyond them to the fellow soul struggling with life at all levels. One can be patient, loving, forgiving and charitable with any tortured, misguided soul.

The law of grace allows for the full manifestation of tenfold return in our lives in a positive way. Simply stated, what goes out from us returns to us tenfold. Kindness will bring ten acts of kindness back to us. So, as we practice the law of grace, we begin to create so much good for ourselves, we will prosper abundantly in all areas of life.

Another delusion I freely admit to is the concept of reincarnation. I have come "to know" that I have lived before in other physical bodies upon this planet. I have remembrances of several incarnations, including as a Greek philosopher, a Native American medicine woman, an Egyptian historian and builder of aqueducts, a French physician's wife gifted in psychic healing, a ship's captain, a German businessman, an English surgeon, and a pre-revolutionary French nobleman. I also "know" I lived in Palestine during the life of Christ, and was healed by him of physical blindness. Memories of these lives have occurred spontaneously, through specific exercises, and by psychic readings or channeled information.

I have observed past-life recall in workshops, in seminars, and in my own work with clients utilizing age regression hypnosis. In the latter work I have facilitated healing of past-life trauma affecting the emotional health of the client in this lifetime.

One client was very fearful of legal authorities and attorneys. The roots of her fear stemmed from being crucified by the Roman authorities, just after witnessing Christ's crucifixion. Unjustly accused and convicted in that life, her fear of injustice was further aggravated by witnessing "God's son" being murdered as well. As a result she also struggled in this life with trusting God and allowing her partnership with God to form.

Reincarnation allows the opportunity for the laws of grace and karma to operate over time. The person who wins the Lotto may be reaping the rewards of charity and kindness dating back to many lifetimes of abundant giving to others at all levels. Seemingly random violence against an innocent victim may be retribution for an act of violence in another time.

Clients who are victims of abusive parents in this lifetime have discovered in age regression hypnosis they did the same as a parent before. They also recognize the lesson inherent in going through the same experience they perpetrated on another. Thus, they now experienced the hurt and pain abuse can cause in a child.

A note of caution is necessary here. Not every event is explainable as karmic law operating through reincarnation. Events may also happen simply to provide learning opportunities we are ready for at this time, or may happen for no apparent reason at all.

What about the issue of destiny? It appears at times as though all the events arising in life are the product of destiny. How is it one meets people they have known before in other lifetimes, or seems to inevitably have a particular experience? It does appear that there is some amount of destiny in one's life.

People will often "feel" as though they are meant to follow a certain career, or their life is meant to be lived in a particular way. Certainly the law of cause and effect would suggest destiny as a natural explanation for many events and circumstances. In truth, there is no doubt some events or situations are destined to happen.

However, the greatest gift given to us is the gift of free will. Not even God will intercede and interfere with free will, which does explain why the world is filled with evil and destructive behavior. At any time we are free to choose the course of our life. While destiny may require the presence of a few situations we must face in this lifetime, most situations and events are subject to free will.

In order to be Co-Creators with God, we are given free will to experience, to know, and ultimately to choose to be at one with God. Humanity hasn't always chosen wisely, accounting for the seeming evil in the world. Many free will choices lead to much of the destructive behavior we see about us. Our destiny may be to do great good in a particular area of endeavor, but instead we choose another path, or choose mediocrity instead of greatness.

The combination of destiny and free will creates the multitudinous probabilities existing for each individual and for the planet as a whole. Humanity collectively experiences this combination of free will and destiny.

It is the destiny of this planet and humanity to move back into fourth dimensional awareness, although if mass consciousness were to continue with negative- and fear-based emotions, our free will choices collectively may prevent this from happening. How and when the shift to fourth dimensional reality finally occurs is subject to the free will choices of all. This is why prophecy changes, since psychic awareness at any one point in time is based on the strongest probability of what will manifest.

As more of humanity increases in awareness so that collective consciousness manifests peace and love, some of the dire predictions for the end of this century can be and already are modified. The severity of the transition which is occurring is already lessening. We can have a peaceful transition to the new golden age. It is up to all of us, individually and collectively. Don't underestimate the power of your thoughts. Collective meditations for peace have created tremendous progress in altering future outcomes. Even coming Earth changes can occur more gradually and less cataclysmically if we work to create peace and harmony amongst ourselves and with Mother Nature.

Some angelic sources suggest this planet has already shifted to the fourth dimension. The free will choice each of us may face is moving to fourth dimensional awareness with this planet, or moving on to other third dimensional worlds, for we will no longer be able to continue on this planet in third dimensional bodies.

Life isn't a set course, but our path is one of multitudinous probabilities based on the free will choices we continually make along the way. Each probability will bring the serendipitous experiences we need, based on the previous choices, so we can continue to learn, grow and become increasingly aware. Free will gives you choices. Choice is there because you deserve the best. You demand the best by choosing.

The most radical delusion I have to offer you is the belief we choose our life's agenda and pattern before we are born, while still in the spirit realm. I believe at the soul level we choose our lifetime, and all its probabilities before we accept this incarnation. The choices are made to have the experiences which will facilitate awareness, resolve past issues, resolve all karma, and learn additional lessons which facilitate our soul's growth and development so we can ultimately become Co-Creators with God.

We choose our curriculum. Only we are responsible for this curriculum and how we respond to it. When we "get" here, and "forget" we chose these probabilities, it is easy to blame and externalize. However, the truth is we chose our experiences and the probabilities which emerge in our lives.

When I make a mistake and experience the consequences I now ask two questions. I ask the same when adversity and misfortune arise. The first question is, how is this here to bless me? The second question is, why did I choose this experience or situation? By seeking awareness to these questions I create new understanding for these events in my life, and thus can move forward in a more positive direction.

When I learned about my diabetes, a situation I interestingly always feared might arise in my life, the answers to these two questions helped me to begin self-healing at every level. When I learned the genetic encodement for diabetes was placed within me, with my permission, to provide me with a hurdle that would facilitate learning, understanding and awareness I could make a different choice about how I responded to this hurdle.

As I asked how my entitled neighbors are there to bless me, and why I chose this experience, I increasingly developed patience and healing awareness which will serve me in all areas of my life. A future chapter is devoted to the situation with these neighbors.

I am learning not to judge others or myself, but to lovingly accept what I have judged in others and in myself. I am increasingly learning how to respond to others in my life and the events that unfold with them with patience and forgiveness.

As part of forgiveness, I learned to visualize a golden light around me, around the other person I am in conflict with, and then ask for the solution to the conflict which is for the highest good of everyone concerned. Ultimately, by simply asking why I chose to have each experience, I can accept it and use it to transform my life, rather than to have an excuse for not taking responsibility for my adventure.

Life will present you with the same lessons over and over again until you meet that lesson. If it is difficult to assert yourself, and you continually choose passivity, life will keep presenting you with challenges to help you choose assertiveness. If you harbor racial or ethnic prejudice, life will continually present you with challenges to resolve that prejudice. If you resent authority, you will continually face authoritarian experiences until you learn how to handle authority effectively and how to discriminate and respond to different authority. Whatever you fear you will continually face until that lesson is resolved. No matter what the challenge is, it will continually come to you, until you deal with it.

The bad news is, once you resolve a lesson you will get a new one. The good news is, true joy and happiness emerge as we meet the challenges that are given. As previously stated we are not on this planet to have a vacation! Once a challenge is met, new ones will come.

Ultimately we are here to experience all aspects of life in the physical, to know the emotions that go with all aspects of physicality, so we can become Co-Creators with God. In the eternal tapestry of life, being spiritual beings having a human experience, we experience all to unify all. The task in the physical dimensions is to unify the human ego with our spirit, creating a true partnership with our Source. Each experience and situation provides the opportunity for ego and spirit to unite in one whole.

Ruth P. Freeman writes in *Each Day A New Beginning*, for the Hazelden Meditation services, each day provides its own gifts. She writes:

> "We are guaranteed experiences that are absolutely right for us today. We are progressing on schedule. Even when our personal hopes are unmet, we are given the necessary opportunities for achieving those goals that complement our unique destinies.
>
> Today is full of special surprises, and we will be the recipient of the ones which are sent to help us grow—in all the ways necessary for our continued recovery. We might not consider every experience a gift at this time. But hindsight will offer the clarity lacking at the moment, just as it has done in many instances that have gone before.
>
> We are only offered part of our personal drama each day. But we can trust our lives to have many scenes, many acts, points of climax, and a conclusion. Each of us tells a story with our lives, one different from all other stories too. The days ahead will help us tell our story. Our interactions with others will influence our outcomes and theirs. We can trust the drama and give fully to our roles.
>
> **Every day is a gift exchange.
> I give, and I will receive."**

Ultimately, we are here to learn to give and to receive love. It is all we take with us when we leave this planet. All laws and all experiences are here to learn this, so we can manifest it unconditionally in all situations. Since God is Love, our full partnership with God is in giving and receiving love.

We actually live in a world which can function as a seven

dimensional world. Humanity has believed in the limitations of three dimensional experience. In limited awareness, we only want to believe in three dimensions. Three dimensional awareness, part of the historical period, has been a necessary step in the evolution of humanity. As humanity rises in consciousness we are returning to higher dimensional awareness and functioning.

Many masters have come to us throughout the historical period, and taught a greater understanding, a greater awareness, of dimensions beyond. Some of my delusions I have shared with you are part of this greater dimensional awareness. Increasing numbers of humanity are moving back into fourth dimensional awareness while in the physical. Higher dimensional awareness will allow humanity to co-create the physical universe. I believe this is about to occur on a massive scale.

We are all here now to be a part of this grand adventure. As we come to understand all the basic truths which operate in this universe, with awareness we can apply these allowing for alignment and harmony with all that is good. Understanding basic, universal principles and applying them in our lives, allows us to more easily and effectively traverse the path of joy.

CHAPTER SIX

MISSION

Have you wondered why you are here, on this planet, at this point in time and space? Have you wondered what the meaning and purpose of life is, and further, whether you have a special role to fulfill as part of your life? Do you find yourself wondering about this more at some times than you do at other times? Perhaps your purpose or mission was trying to reveal itself to you, to enter into your conscious awareness.

We all have reasons to be here. Each of us has a special mission or role to fulfill, as well as larger missions or purposes to achieve. We have general missions and purposes for being on this planet, in addition to our particular part in the grand plan. Part of adventurous living is discovering and fulfilling all these missions, specific and general. As we understand our missions and put them into action, we naturally begin to experience joy and adventure.

Mission or purpose can manifest itself in myriad ways, whether we have just one set purpose in life, or many missions or purposes for ourselves. We also have many missions to others and to the collective whole, within the larger context of the planetary experience. We have to discover what our missions are, then enact these missions in the world about us.

To begin with, each of us has a special purpose, or unique mission to bring to our life. God created each and everyone of us with special talents and abilities in order to contribute to the overall pattern of life and to the divine plan.

Talents and abilities are not limited to only those qualities which contribute to vocational pursuits, although these are important and in keeping with our divine purpose. Nor are vocational skills and abilities restricted, for purposes of mission, to those the world currently values. For in the eyes of God, all vocational pursuits are worthy. The waitress and the trash hauler are just as important as the genetic scientist discovering how life itself manifests.

Each of us has a vital part to play in the ongoing evolution of life. For all of us are part of the greater oneness of life on this planet. To let even one life waste away is tragic, as each one is meant to contribute to the greater whole, to the greater good.

Even seemingly evil and destructive roles can contribute to the whole, by providing experiences all of us need to gain understanding through having those experiences or through observing their harmful effects. While regrettable, these negative roles allow us to distinguish between good and evil, light and darkness. However, we do not have to learn the hard way, and we can choose to eliminate destructive and evil roles from this planet.

For our special purpose, talents and abilities include all those traits which manifest for us in the unique and special ways they emerge in and through us. In addition to specific vocational talents, they include our capacity to demonstrate and communicate love, patience, forgiveness and long-suffering.

They include our special ability to express our personality and its traits with others. They are our ability to solve problems, work with others and instill our values in others. They are our ability to nurture others, whether as a friend, parent, grandparent, lover, spouse, volunteer, coach, co-worker or humanitarian.

They are our ability to take care of our part of the world, to grow things, to manifest beauty and to heal our planetary home. They are our ability to bring joy and happiness to our community, to bring peace, to bring prosperity and to bring hope to the world. They are our capacity to manifest healing physically, mentally, emotionally and spiritually to ourselves and to others.

Each of us has been given a special mission by God, a unique role we fulfill during our current lifetime. When we are conceived, this special mission is encoded within us, within our very DNA structure, and begins to manifest from the day we are born. The encodement provides us with all the probabilities we require to manifest our divine mission during our lifetime.

As we grow, we begin to discover these probabilities and begin to make choices that help us to bring our divine mission into being. As we grow older we begin to refine this process to achieve purpose. We also become increasingly aware of our divine mission, helping to ensure its success.

Allow me to share the example of my son as he neared his twelfth birthday. For the last three years he has talked about being an attorney when he pursues his career. He is very smart, and other kids are forever suggesting he should be a physician or politician, but he says "no" because he wants to be an attorney. He is very interested in movies and novels about legal issues and likes to see how attorneys work. At career day he went to a session with an attorney. He has a sense of fairness, and is concerned about injustice and righting the wrongs of the world. He is very argumentative, and states his case forcefully. Before he was born both of us "knew" to name him Justin, which is Latin for justice. I suspect his divine mission has to do with a legal career, although he is young and other potential missions may yet emerge.

My wife also serves as an example as she is an elementary educator. She always had a strong interest in, and passion for, teaching. Even when she considered psychology for a time, she eventually came back to teaching. She currently struggles with only substitute teaching and tutoring children, as she awaits her opportunity to fulfill her divine mission on a full time basis in her own classroom. Although frustrated at not having her own classroom yet, her desire remains and mission is fulfilled in many classrooms a day at a time. Hopefully she will have an opportunity to begin her mission soon.

If not, with some of the probable changes coming on this planet, her mission may be in helping establish a new educational system as civilization transforms itself. Even if she is detoured currently, being an educator will assist her in whatever her divine mission is at that time. For always, everything is in divine order in her life, and in all of our lives.

For myself, I have always "known" that I would be involved in healing others. As a teen, others naturally turned to me for counsel and advice. As college progressed I became more and more interested in psychology, particularly more innovative therapeutic approaches. As my career progresses, it is increasingly clear to me one of my missions is to provide healing through the practice of psychology. This encompasses healing at the physical, mental, emotional and spiritual levels, to be innovative, and to bring forward new technology as I have begun to do.

A strong sense of teaching is also present for me. I started out wanting to be a teacher, have taught graduate and undergraduate psychology courses, and have learned how to facilitate seminars. I "know" part of my mission is to teach, providing healing through that process as well. As I finalize this manuscript, the opportunity to be a facilitator for a seminar enterprise has "come" into my life.

Further, I have a strong interest in "writing" and now "know" I am on a divine mission to write, to further disseminate ideas and healing technology. Besides writing this book, I have also submitted an article on "vision hypnosis" to a local publication. These examples show how divine mission begins to manifest in our lives.

How is it that we begin to understand what our divine mission or purpose is? How do we begin to discover and understand what we are here to do and to learn while we are in this physical incarnation? What lessons are we here to learn so we can facilitate the growth and development of our souls and also other souls? How do we begin to understand what the specific plan is for us as we live in the world?

There are many ways we can begin to understand what God's plan is for us. Speaking to God with purposeful prayer, asking that His will be done in and through us each and every day is a good place to begin. To begin listening to the "still, small voice" within so that we can be guided to right action in fulfilling our part of the divine plan is an important first step. For God does speak to us, often intuitively, or by signs we learn to attend to.

Often messages and guidance comes in dreams. Then too, guidance comes from the seeming coincidences discussed earlier which, when properly understood, lead us in the right direction. Use of extrasensory perception and skills, what is often called "psychic" ability, can often lead us to understand divine will in our lives. Seeking this information from others more skilled in psychic ability can also lead us to right action and guidance. While all of us have varying degrees of psychic ability, sometimes guidance may be sought from others who have developed their ability until such time as we are able to use our own abilities.

One of the most powerful and effective ways of ascertaining divine wisdom, whether this comes to us from our own higher self, our spirit guides, angelic beings, discarnate entities who also wish to be helpful, or from God himself, is through meditation on a daily basis. First, meditation recharges our spiritual energy. More importantly, meditation allows God to speak to us directly, often guiding us to right action and to the fulfillment of His plan in our lives. Often this manifests in very practical guidance day to day.

Divine purpose can also be learned through work in growth seminars, as well as in a variety of individual or small group healing and facilitation experiences. These can be anything from Bible study groups to support groups, therapeutic body massage and body work to metaphysical training experiences. Search for God study groups sponsored by the Association of Research and Enlightenment can be another source of learning. Working with a life chiropractic practitioner or other holistic healers may be another source of learning. Often we are guided to just the "right" experience or situation that allows for us to understand better our divine mission and purpose.

Attending to our own talents and abilities, likes and dislikes, helps us to understand our role in life. Assessing these abilities and talents as we go along helps us to choose the career, action and behavior with which we are meant to be of service.

Sometimes a particular job only provides us with material needs so we can best be of service in other areas that are not rewarded financially. Not all jobs or careers have status or high monetary value, yet all are necessary and may fulfill divine mission or offer a lesson, timely to our growth and development.

Learning to discern our mission means attending to our urges and where they lead us. Yet, we may also end up where we did not think we wanted to be, and we have to discover how this experience is beneficial to us, so that our overall mission is fulfilled. Sometimes the seeming detours are necessary paths along the way.

While our mission may include our career path or occupational choice, our overall mission or purpose is much larger than this. Career or job may serve little or no use to our overall mission, but simply provide a means so we can fulfill our larger purpose. What each of us needs to know is that each of us has a special mission or purpose. To thwart that purpose, to ignore it or to go against it only harms us, leads to great suffering and prolonging our journey back to God.

One of our greatest challenges is aligning our will and purpose with divine will and purpose. Many of us attempt to avoid this, fearing we will lose our identity if we surrender to God's Will for us. We use our egos to Ease God Out of our lives, falsely believing we preserve our integrity by going it alone. This is one interpretation of "original sin" or rebellion from God, as we choose to go it alone and forsake our Heavenly Father-Mother.

In reality we do not lose our identity, nor our integrity and our individuality, by embracing God's Will and attuning our will to His Will. The truth is we enhance ourselves when we embrace our oneness with God and with all creation, including all of humanity, with no exceptions. This means embracing those we perceive as the most despicable amongst us, in love and grace, not approving of their reprehensible behavior, but seeing beyond it to the truth and beauty within, the Christ Consciousness, the divinity within that links them with the Creator just as it links us with the Creator.

When we attune our will to divine will we forge a true partnership with God. Surrendering our will does not mean we become subservient to God, but rather that in partnership we accept the greater Wisdom and Love that always knows the better choice, the better course of action. We do not lose our free will, but enhance it as we access greater Truth and Love. We retain our free will, now making choices which the benefit of greater Wisdom has to offer.

Our mission may be singular or multi-faceted. We may have many missions, within the context of one, or a few greater missions. Missions may change as our lives progress. Understanding and making the most of our mission becomes our immediate and daily task.

Since I believe part of my mission is to provide healing, I take every opportunity to provide healing, not just in my professional work but in all situations. A kind word of encouragement and guidance to an acquaintance is just as important as the most significant, intense individual therapy session I conduct. Making life easier for a frustrated driver, and this has been a real challenge for me, demonstrating cooperation and mutual respect, is just as important as saving a troubled marriage.

Each of us is a necessary and important strand we add to the entire fabric of life and creation right now. A seemingly modest role of waitressing can become a mission of love and service in which customers feel like honored and special guests. Is it not wonderful when we have this experience with our waitress when she is coming from her joy? A seemingly demeaning job of collecting trash or sweeping floors can become a mission of love and service creating and maintaining a clean, healthy and beautiful environment for all of us to enjoy and share.

Beyond our particular individual mission are other missions, other areas to be at service to the world at large, humanity in general, and God's plan for this planet and this universe. As each of us contributes by and through our mission we all contribute by and to the ongoing progress, development and evolution of humanity overall.

A general mission on this planet is simply to learn and to grow, physically, mentally, emotionally and spiritually. As already stated planet Earth is a classroom in the universe. We "attend" this classroom to learn lessons. Some of these include learning and appreciating differences, learning to live in physicality, learning to understand a dualistic reality (yin and yang, good and evil, light and darkness, masculine and feminine), learning not to judge, learning universal law, and learning how to be Co-Creators with God, to name only a few.

Another general mission is to positively contribute to the specific and overall quality of our relationships. We are here to create meaningful, joyful and positive relationships with others. We are here to extend love unconditionally to all we meet, whether a spouse, parent, child, friend, neighbor or stranger. This does not mean accepting dislikable behavior, but we do not have to respond to these behaviors with condemnation, disdain, and other negative or fear-based emotions.

Jesus taught us to love God, and to love others as we love

God. In his life he continuously demonstrated unconditional love, even having dinner with what was considered to be the most despicable of the society in his day, the tax collectors. He loved even the money changers in the temple, although he still had to clear them out. Most remarkably, he demonstrated this truth as he loved and forgave his tormentors on the way to being crucified. He did not make any exceptions. He has expected no less from each of us.

Patience, love and understanding are the missions in our relationships. As we give love we receive love back. As I stated before, the only thing we take with us when we leave this planet is the love we give and receive.

Loving and forbearance of others begins with giving love and forgiveness to ourselves. For we cannot truly extend love to others until we do so to ourselves. From there we need to extend our love to our spouses or significant others, family members, friends, neighbors, and even to our enemies. We demonstrate this love by kindness, commitment, patience and giving of ourselves. Our love manifests in our intention with others, our commitment to give our very best to them. It can be as simple as a small act of kindness, to smiling instead of reacting to the enraged driver saluting us with her raised middle finger, and to being calm when facing rude behavior.

Self-righteous anger and indignation are the antithesis here. Even if you are "justified" in telling another person off, all you really succeed in doing is provoking rage in him/her, not understanding nor a corrective course of action. Only in movies or in soap operas does telling someone off lead to awareness. Only actors say thanks for kicking me in the butt, now I see the light, now I will become transformed.

With children we have a special mission to be loving and nurturing. We do not own children, for they are souls entrusted to our care by God. They are a sacred responsibility, for we are to nurture them, teach and guide them, provide loving discipline, and instill values in them so that they can learn, grow and contribute to the greater good, the greater harmony of humankind.

Another general mission is to "be" an example to others as we demonstrate love, compassion, understanding and wisdom. As we live joy, as we let our inner wisdom emerge in our own lives, we demonstrate truth to others. It is what we do, not what we say. It is walking the walk. All of us have witnessed the hypocrisy of those who want to tell us how to live, but who do not want to live their own lessons.

This is not to be confused with perfection, for each of us has our flaws and those moments when we do not live up to our ideals. There is a difference between those who say, "do as I say not as I do," versus those that say this is a way that works, this leads to greater awareness, even as they struggle to do the same themselves.

These days we like to tear down people for not being perfect in every area of their lives, especially if they are leaders or are in the public spotlight. The confusion comes from blending the messenger with the message. It is the message that is important! However, as the messenger tries to live the message, often imperfectly, a greater wisdom and awareness of truth principles can come forward, even as they struggle themselves to live the message.

Finally, a general mission is to make our "own little corner of the world" a better place to be. As we move forward in service, as we work to make where we are at each moment in time a better place, we improve all of the world. If the seeds of war begin with an angry thought toward another that is allowed to fester, then the seeds of peace and harmony also begin as peace is allowed to manifest in thought, word and deed with others. Have prosperity by giving to others. Have peace by teaching peace to others. Practice vigilance for God and His Kingdom by honoring and keeping the Ten Commandments, in thought, word and deed.

There is a hymn called "The Greatest Thing" which goes like this:

> The greatest thing in all my life is knowing You.
> The greatest thing in all my life is knowing You.
> I want to know You more;
> I want to know You more;
> The greatest thing in all my life is knowing You.
>
> The greatest thing in all my life is loving You.

The greatest thing in all my life is loving You.
I want to love You more;
I want to love You more;
The greatest thing in all my life is loving You.

The greatest thing in all my life is serving You.
The greatest thing in all my life is serving You.
I want to serve You more;
I want to serve You more;
The greatest thing in all my life is serving You.

Ultimately, mission is summarized in this hymn of knowing, loving and serving God. As we do this, we manifest our mission at this point in time, space and place. As we understand all our missions we increasingly lead adventurous lives, create joy, and bring joy to the world.

CHAPTER SEVEN

KNOWING GOD'S PLAN FOR US

There is a divine plan for the universe, and for this planet. This plan unfolds taking into consideration all probabilities of all free will choices of all beings on all dimensional levels. An omniscient God is certainly capable of allowing free will to operate and yet also allow His divine plan to unfold toward desirable outcomes. Within this context there is some destiny, but destiny is not absolute. Outcomes may vary as the plan emerges, due to free will choices.

There is a divine plan for this planet. According to the Archangel Metatron, the universe is currently in a twenty year period known as the still space between the outbreath and the inbreath of God. It is a period which affords a unique opportunity for this planet and for humanity on this planet. The experiment we are currently undergoing is to accomplish mass ascension of this planet and this species gently through a change in consciousness rather than through cataclysmic change. The latter has been the usual way mass ascension has been accomplished for other third dimensional worlds.

Ascension is the process whereby we move from third dimensional to higher dimensional realities and functioning. It is one of the lessons taught by Jesus through the process of resurrection. He demonstrated death could be overcome, and subsequently left third dimensional reality through ascension.

We are capable of achieving ascension without having to experience physical death. We can literally transform our bodies into light bodies operating at higher dimensional levels, through a change in consciousness, practicing love and forgiveness, and forming a partnership with God in which we attune our will to His will.

Part of the divine plan is to accomplish ascension on a massive scale during this transitional time in this universe. Those of us in physicality get to participate in and create this ascension process, individually and collectively. We can choose individually and collectively to participate in this creation. We will either do this gently and peacefully as we elevate our consciousness, or it will be accomplished without us through cataclysmic changes, natural disasters and destructive forces such as war unleashed by a lack of change in consciousness.

If a sufficient number of us change our thinking to peaceful, collective, creative consciousness then the ascension will occur gently. The Earth, as a sentient being, has already entered fourth dimensional reality, according to Metatron.

Our purpose and mission, individually and collectively, is to help the divine plan unfold peacefully, creating the thousand years of peace promised in the Bible. As we create our lives as masterpieces of joy, as we heal at all levels, and as we live life adventurously we help to fulfill the divine plan.

Each one of us has a vital, instrumental role to play in creating the "new golden age," the thousand years of peace promised for so long. Each of us has the opportunity to help create a new reality of peace, understanding and harmony on a planetary level. Each of us has the opportunity to again become guardians of this planet, maintaining harmony and balance, working with Lady Gaia, Mother Earth.

How do we begin to know and understand God's plan for us? How do we begin to recognize our divine mission and purpose? How do we gain greater awareness of who we are and our part in the tapestry of life, especially in these interesting times?

There are many ways we understand our role in the plan, all of which lead to greater awareness as life unfolds for us. As we access any and all of the many ways Wisdom reveals itself, we begin to understand what our part is in the divine plan set before us.

James Dillet Freeman wrote, "It must have been a happy moment when God created love. When it came forth life itself came with it." He conceives of God as an "infinite and joyous expression of Himself, who came one day to the point in space and time where when he said, Let there be . . . what came into being was you."

God didn't just create us, then leave us on our own, even when our free will choices led us away from God and our partnership with Him. Since He is within us, He has never abandoned us. With free will, we are able to choose what we do with life at any particular moment, and can choose to renew our life at any particular moment, and can choose to renew our partnership with Him.

There are no personalities, there is only God in Action at every point. We are God in Action. When we form a partnership with this God force within us, we then manifest the perfect plan for our lives, for the planet, and for the universe.

The Unity statement of being sums up this truth, as follows:

God is all
Both invisible and visible.
One Presence, One Mind, One Power is all.
This One that is all is perfect life, perfect love, and perfect substance.
I am an individualized expression of God.
I am ever one with This perfect life, perfect love, and perfect substance.

When we accept being one with God, and choose to follow our part in the divine plan, tremendous joy and fulfillment result.

Being one with God's plan is not submission, it is partnership. It is choosing to align our will with divine will. This partnership allows us to be Co-Creators with God, allowing His greater awareness to guide and direct us in right action.

One of the ways we discover God's plan for us is through prayer. All religious and spiritual traditions teach about prayer. Prayer is our opportunity to speak to God directly, to let Him know our needs and wants. Ultimately what we need to ask for in prayer is to become aware, learning how we shall fulfill our divine purpose. Prayer asking for certain things or specific outcomes is very limiting, restricting us to the narrowest view of the plan, or keeping us from knowing the plan at all.

Effective prayer is simply letting God know we are available and ready to participate in our partnership with Him. Part of the Lord's Prayer is "thy Will be done, on Earth as it is in Heaven." Other ways of saying this include "Not my will, but thine, O Lord, be done in me and through me this and every day," and "Mighty I AM presence, take control of my life this and every day." Even as I write, I start out with the simple prayer, "Mighty I AM Presence, take control of this writing."

Prayer is our communication to God. It is about finding our Higher Self. Billie Freeman wrote that finding our "self" is the sincere desire of every heart, the aim and purpose of every life. She states the fulfillment of this desire of the heart, the attaining of this aim and purpose, comes through taking thought through the process of prayer and meditation.

The simplest prayer and meditation is "God is love." This extension of love in us to others becomes a simple but powerful prayer and meditation, to go in love. We are to go into our everyday world, our home, our place of employment, our city, our country, and our world and be our Self, going and being love.

Prayer is wonderfully summed up by this Prayer of an unknown Confederate soldier;

> *I asked for strength, that I might achieve;*
> *I was made weak, that I might learn humbly to obey.*
> *I ask for health that I might do greater things;*
> *I was given infirmity that I might do better things.*
> *I asked for riches that I might be happy;*
> *I was given poverty that I might be wise.*
> *I asked for power that I might have the praise of men;*
> *I was given weakness that I might feel the need of God.*
> *I asked for all things that I might enjoy life;*
> *I was given life that I might enjoy all things.*
> *I got nothing I asked for,*
> *But everything I'd hoped for*
> *Almost despite myself, my unspoken prayers*
> *were answered;*
> *I am among all men, most richly blessed.*

If prayer is communication with God, meditation is communication from God. Meditation allows us to still our minds, so we may know what God wishes to tell us. The mind engages in endless dialogue with itself, an endless chatter which interferes with our ability to hear God speak to us. If this endless chatter centers in fear, doubt and worry, we become even further disconnected from God.

Through meditation we learn to still the mind long enough for communication to come forward. It may be symbols, images, a vision or auditory statements. Guidance can come in many forms, including messages from deceased relatives, spiritual leaders, angels or spirit guides. Sometimes guidance emerges in a thought or feeling, a sensation or a "sudden knowing."

In meditation I become aware of solutions to problems I face, or have sudden insights on how to proceed or how to understand a situation from a different perspective. Sometimes greater awareness emerges, whether about a situation, a relationship, a conflict, or simply where I am at in my life.

There are many meditation traditions to choose from, or you can simply spend time alone stilling your thoughts. There is no one right way to meditate. What is important is regular periods of meditation, done daily. At least 15 minutes per session are needed. Many people find it is helpful to meditate twice a day, preferably at the beginning and end of the day. Many advocate meditating at a regular time. I find it helpful to meditate with music. Numerous recordings facilitate meditation in general, as well as facilitate special kinds of meditation.

Myrtle Fillmore, one of the founders of Unity, wrote about how to gain spiritual understanding, which also serves as an overall guideline to meditation. She said we not only seek to know our part in the divine plan but we also seek to know in greater and greater awareness.

She wrote the first step is to become still and admit there is a need to know, to understand. We are to become like the little child, and not try to display our knowledge and skill in the presence of the Divine Mind. We are to ask for greater understanding. It will work because it is the right way. "Become a little child," spoke Jesus, which is the way to ask for greater awareness.

The second step is to realize we have a Divine faculty given to us called understanding or wisdom. Without it, we would understand the meaning of nothing.

After the existence of the faculty of understanding is acknowledged, she said the next step is to affirm our belief in its fullness and perfection within *us*. We are not to envy another's understanding, not even that of Jesus, but affirm the wholeness and perfection of God's gift of understanding to us. Only belief is needed.

The next step is to become totally nonresistant-totally willing for full of understanding to come into every part of our mind, our imagination, our intellect, our judgment, our memory. We are to be willing for a flood of understanding to surge through our mind—both our conscious and subconscious mind. This attitude of total willingness is the final stage of preparation. It will allow the character of understanding to permeate our mind.

From that point on you will *know*. More and more you will know. Each time you meditate there will be a new awareness in yourself of the "meaning" of whatever knowledge you encounter.

Another pathway to knowing God's plan is through the faculty of intuition. Intuition, our sixth sense, is the part of our mind that just knows what to do. Intuition is our "gut feeling" about something. Our brains are composed of two halves. Intuition is seated in our right brain while reason and logic are seated in our left brain. In the Western world, we have been taught to ignore our intuition, to only function with our reason and logic. Our universities emphasize our left brain functioning. Ram Dass has called universities "temples to the rational mind."

Yet we were created with both sides of our brains. We need to learn how to balance our thinking, using each half, not discarding either. We should not give up reason and logic, we should always question and examine what is presented to us, but intuition also provides a way of knowing and an awareness. Einstein, in a moment of intuitive brilliance and insight, discovered the theory of relativity. He then spent a year using his reason and logic to prove what his intuition already knew.

Out of meditation and intuition, one learns how to listen to the "still, small voice of God within." As we learn to enter the stillness, we gain access to this voice which speaks to us, teaches and guides us, making us more aware. This voice also speaks to us at other times, directing us and guiding us if we but allow ourselves to listen and trust this process.

The "still small voice within" is very practical, guiding us on major decisions or paths of unfoldment in our lives. Several years ago I was anxious to leave a job which had become a negative experience for me. I interviewed to be the director of two outpatient clinics. After meeting with the owner, I believed it was in my best interest to take the new position. Driving back to the hospital I already worked at I clearly heard in my mind, "This is not the job for you. Wait! The right job will come to you."

I didn't want to hear this and unfortunately didn't listen, so I took the position. Within a year I realized I made the wrong choice. The job was a disaster. The owner was a self-centered and angry person who did not keep the promises he made.

The final incident followed attempts to get paid twice monthly instead of monthly. It was announced by memo we would be paid twice a month, beginning the next month. When the first semi-monthly pay was due, there was no check. It was denied the change was ever announced. It became even more clear I worked for a dysfunctional agency. I immediately worked to get out of there.

Subsequently I was better at listening to this voice within. Prior to an automobile trip to Florida one summer, I wanted to buy a minivan, as it would be roomier than the car we owned. I met with a salesperson and made an excellent preliminary deal. Back at the office, alone with the door closed, thinking about getting the minivan, I heard an emphatic "Wait!" I was startled, and looked around expecting to see somebody standing behind me in the room. It was hard heeding the advice of this voice, because I "really" wanted the car. But I was learning to listen, and did not buy the car.

A few weeks later, the clinic I worked for gave me problems paying monies owed me at agreed upon times of the month. If I had ignored the voice, I would have been in trouble financially.

At one time I strongly desired to have a full time position that included benefits, after working two years independently. I prayed, affirmed and visualized this would happen. Before Christmas of that year, I was compelled to attend a past life recall night at the Alhambra Institute, a metaphysical organization.

Even though I worked a long day, it was a busy time of year, and I was tired, I listened to the inner urge to attend this event. As I drove the extra distance out of my way my "still, small voice" said, "Your prayers have been answered."

When my turn came I asked why I was compelled to be there. Alexia, in trance, explained an angel was coming from a great distance with a message for me. She reported the angel hovered before her, information was given to me and it was shared the date of January 17th would be significant. At home that night, tucking my 6 year old son into bed, he looked up at me and said he couldn't wait until January 17th, in no way knowing an angel gave me the same date earlier in the evening. After the 17th I was offered a full time position with benefits, starting the following June, with two weeks of all expenses paid training in San Francisco. I was even offered $5000 more in salary than previously discussed.

When I felt frustrated and disappointed about the director job mentioned earlier, I sensed the next regional meeting in Indianapolis was going to culminate in further disappointment and possible demotion for me. As I drove to the airport my "still, small voice within" told me not to worry. The voice said, "It is not your time yet, your time will come." It gave me great comfort then, and for several months after, as that situation worsened.

Dreams may also provide us with direction about God's plan for us, although often in ways that are not readily clear at first. The Bible frequently mentions the use of dreams providing guidance to others, whether Joseph when imprisoned in Egypt, the Pharaoh in the same story warning of the coming drought, or another Joseph being warned to take Mary and the infant Jesus out of Israel.

Dreams may provide either direct guidance or disguised guidance. The latter requires us to discern the direction the dream is suggesting. Dream interpretation, based on common knowledge of symbols combined with an intuitive feel for what each element of the dream means, can provide the guidance needed. Often the intuitive meaning can be discerned by being each part of the dream, discovering what each part is thinking or feeling. The answers provide overall clues to the meaning and guidance contained within each dream.

Direction and guidance may also be assessed through the use of psychic gifts, whether our own or from others. Consulting psychics, using tarot cards or other forms of divination, astrology, numerology, Viking Runes, angel cards or Native American animal cards can help provide answers or directions. Alexia, a gifted psychic I know, states "the future is not meant to be left to chance." She also reminds us these sources of information, like all others, require us to trust our own intuitive feeling about the messages received, as well as the "sources" of the messages. Alexia reminds seekers of Jesus' admonition, "you shall know them by their works."

Hypnosis can also serve as a gateway to inner knowledge or awareness. Hypnosis allows us to access the subconscious mind, where all memory and awareness resides, as well as the Superconscious Mind, which is our access to our Higher Self, our inner Wisdom. I have clients in hypnotic trance speak with angels, spirit guides or ascended masters. One woman even received messages from a loving orange light that provided her with needed information as she faced major surgery.

Following a particular religion or spiritual tradition may also proved guidance or direction. All religious or spiritual traditions have within them at their core spiritual truth or wisdom. By following and practicing a religion or spiritual tradition one can be on a path of increasing awareness that allows their divine plan to unfold to them. Spiritual traditions such as major religious faiths, as well as Alcoholics Anonymous, Narcotics Anonymous and related groups provide many with a path that allows them to manifest their divine plan. I have watched inner city, fourth generation welfare recipients addicted to crack begin to follow NA and actively work the 12-step recovery program. As they do this their lives are transformed, opportunities for work and education "suddenly" materialize, and their divine plan begins to manifest.

James Dillet Freeman writes how Unity teachers often state that God has a plan for us. God made us with vast potential. God's plan for us is to grow to fulfill that potential, to be all we are meant to be. Part of that potential is freedom to find our way to our fulfillment. This is one of the greatest gifts that life has given us.

Failure and past suffering can also direct us to an awareness of God's plan. Rather than being defeated by a failure or suffering, these can challenge us and motivate us to do even greater things. I failed with a client who became angry and hurt when I was not careful with confidentiality to a third party who referred her to me. Caught up in the excitement of our work together and the discoveries emerging with each session, I began to view her more as a colleague and co-adventurer rather than simply as a client in need of alleviating suffering and fear in her life. I allowed my ego to get in the way of being of service to her. It was very painful to recognize my error, my failure to be focused with her and to be of service to her.

In my failure and the suffering I endured at not achieving my ideal with her, I learned to set my ego aside, to remember with other clients to be more focused, to be a better listener, and to remind myself I was there to serve them first no matter what other learning or discovery took place. Being challenged by failure and learning from failure can guide us back to God's plan for us, letting God guide and provide.

To trust and allow means letting our Inner Wisdom speak to us and direct us. This can come in the many ways outlined above. Learning to trust our Inner Wisdom, to listen to our "still, small voice within," to see that all events offer us wisdom and guidance, allows our partnership with God to operate in our lives. For then we truly know God's plan for us.

Understanding there is a master plan, as well as our part in the plan as it continually unfolds, helps us to live adventurously and with joy. As we then move into action and apply universal truths, we enter the path of joy and create our lives as masterpieces of joy.

We are living in exciting times for we have the opportunity to help create and manifest the divine plan for Earth and humanity. Each of us has a key part to play in the unfoldment of this plan. Be part of the adventure of transforming Earth and humanity, achieving mass ascension peacefully and harmoniously, while learning joy for yourself.

PART TWO

APPLYING BASIC TRUTHS

TO ACHIEVE JOY

CHAPTER EIGHT

ENTITLED NEIGHBORS

As we understand the wisdom and universal laws of this universe we can apply this knowledge in all circumstances to create joy in our lives. As I have emphasized in the first part of the book, even painful realities and adversities become opportunities for learning, growth and development to take place. Adversities become challenging adventures which ultimately serve our highest good.

As we turn these stumbling blocks into stepping stones for our greater good, we create the path of joy in our lives, although in the moment we may not experience much, if any, joy. In facing and positively dealing with adversity and challenge, we overcome negative and fear-based emotions and learn to manifest positive and love-based emotions.

One of the more challenging adventures I faced in the past four years is the entitled neighbors who live right next door. Every neighborhood has a family like this one. Their sense of entitlement is such that they are totally self-absorbed and self-centered. As such, they are oblivious to the effects of their behavior on others. Further, they do not follow local ordinances and subdivision covenants, let alone the social norms and customs that others generally and informally agree upon. Most try to live by these informal rules so everyone may enjoy peace and comfort in their own homes.

However, in every neighborhood there is one family or household that neither understands or cares what these rules of conduct are, nor do they understand the limitations imposed by property boundaries. These are the families that act as though they were living out in the country on spacious acreage, yet are residing in the midst of a subdivision, community or city.

Unfortunately for us, the entitled family in our neighborhood lives next to us. Ironically, when we first moved in they were very friendly and were glad to have us as their new neighbors. There were no problems at first, although other neighbors warned us about their behavior. However, it was not long before the friendliness disappeared, and this family became a major challenge and adversity in my life.

Facing this ongoing challenge is difficult, to say the least. Yet the lessons learned along the way, and the surprising ways this situation is gradually resolving itself over time, illustrate how applying universal truths leads to manifesting joy.

When we first looked at our present house, one of these neighbors was visiting the previous owners as we looked at our home for the first time. She called out in surprise and delight when she saw me, as we knew each other previously. Due to the prior association, the family was delighted when we moved in, welcomed us warmly, and we became regular visitors at each others' homes.

However, warning signs appeared almost immediately. They spoke about conflict with the neighbors behind, claiming others didn't tolerate her children's behavior, or any "normal" family noise. The neighbors behind, in turn, told us of their problems with the family next door. It was hard to tell who was being truthful, and we gave everyone the benefit of the doubt.

On New Year's Eve, the first year in our new home, we discovered who the problem neighbors were. At ten minutes to midnight we heard a loud commotion outside, and found milling teens angrily yelling, swearing and fighting next door to us and in our front yard. The adolescent sons were left home alone, and a major party was taking place. Most of the teens on the lawn of our house and their driveway appeared intoxicated or high.

My wife ran out of the house to intervene while I called the police. She immediately stopped one young man from beating another in the head with a shovel. When I got outside this man was lying unconscious on the lawn. Miraculously, he disappeared with the aid of his friends as the police finally arrived. We later learned another individual chased someone with an axe from their wood pile. Earlier, several young people urinated off the back deck or behind trees in the yard, completely unaware they were in full view of the neighbors behind.

Before the police arrived several neighbors intervened and

prevented serious harm from happening to anyone else, let alone their own property. During this, both sons were extremely rude with the neighbors, and especially toward my wife.

With the arrival of the police the crowd disappeared rapidly and within moments it looked like nothing ever went on. Long before the parents returned home all evidence of a rowdy party was completely gone. Most amazingly, especially considering how frequently these neighbors throw their garbage on the ground rather than in a container, the yard was immaculate the next morning.

Initially the police didn't take action, but after the insistence of the immediate neighbors, a ticket was subsequently issued to the older son for providing alcohol to minors. With a well rehearsed story for their parents, everybody else must have lied about what happened, because the parents didn't believe the neighbors, including the gentleman on the other side who remains on friendly terms with them.

An attempt was made by many to express concerns about the incident. I attempted to mediate a meeting between the mother and several neighbors, without success. She later stated to me on the phone, "I'm not calling you a liar, but I have to believe my sons." What goes around comes around, and ironically, the very same words were spoken to her by the father of a family friend when he allegedly stole money from her purse.

Within a few months time it was very clear we lived next door to what appears to be a typical dysfunctional family. The father appears to be an alcoholic and doesn't seem to be involved as a parent. He is constantly criticized by his wife, especially in front of others, and with particular malice when his business failed and he was unemployed for a period of time. Even now his wife screams at him outside, belittling him in full view of the neighborhood.

The children are elevated to peer status by the mother, replacing the husband's role in the family. Few, if any, limits are imposed on the children, and often they are rewarded for misbehavior or failure. The oldest son's reward for hosting an unchaperoned and violent party was to take a new car to college.

The next older son apparently has a reputation for fighting and allegedly has had assault charges brought against him previously. Both sons have a reputation for troublesome behavior, which not coincidentally, we learned about from a variety of sources. Yet the mother sincerely believes they are good kids and others malign them for no reason. Even so, she often asks for advice about how to deal with her sons, none of which she follows anyway.

The oldest daughter acts as the family spokesperson, often inappropriately challenging adults perceived to be enemies of the family. She tries to stare us down, but knows better than to say anything to us directly. She has challenged adults living behind her, though, questioning their complaints about loud behavior late at night or complaints about their dogs barking incessantly or leaving their business on others' lawns. The youngest daughter appears to be a sad and perhaps lonely child, who was initially the most friendly with us, and who was most bothered by the emerging hostility.

The family also seems to be loose with the truth, learned well from the mother who appears to chronically lie. She tells different neighbors different versions of the same event. For instance, that New Year's night she told us she was at a concert at the Palace, yet told others she was close by at another party. She claimed her sister supervised another party the second son tried to have only two months later, when we knew she was not there until very late.

As in all dysfunctional families, members act out and misbehave, but rally against the outsiders who object or set limits on inappropriate conduct. These families also create conflict with others, no doubt unconsciously, as a way to diffuse the tension which inevitably arises between them. There will be seeming quiet and peace for awhile, until provocative behavior emerges again. They lay low for awhile, until another episode occurs. Since we are learning not to respond to the provocations, they now more often end up in conflict with one another.

Of course, it wasn't long after the first incident before there was another episode, despite clear warnings another drunken brawl would not be acceptable. Two months later, the parents and daughters left to attend the family weekend at the college the oldest son was attending at the time. This left the younger son home alone, and he was going to have a party. This time, as soon as the cars started arriving next door, we joined other neighbors in calling the police

As we waited for the police, working with a Sergeant familiar with the previous problem and this family in general, we counted 14 teens suddenly leave before the patrol car arrived. Todays' suburban teens are highly sophisticated and sometimes use police scanners. Fortunately this time, possible later problems were thwarted before they could develop. The neighbor's sister appeared later that night and the mother tried to claim she was there the whole night.

When the mother returned home she called to irately complain to my wife, as if we would back down from setting limits as promised before we would do. She complained about us "calling the police on her son every time we are away." Naturally, what the neighbors and adults said was irrelevant, and only the son was believable.

The same day I confronted the son about his behavior and his previous rude behavior with my wife. Unfortunately, I chose to say to him I wasn't "dumb" enough to believe his lies like his mother, which gave him an excuse to storm away muttering threats. Escalating myself, I suggested to him I could make his life miserable if he wanted to take me on.

When there is conflict with someone else, it is so easy for it to escalate into a cycle of self-righteous, vindictive behavior on both sides. With entitled neighbors, who have little or no regard for others and no sense of boundaries, it was easy for the conflict to escalate. The sons and older daughter were especially ready to create turmoil, since they could then externalize blame for the conflict.

Remarks and "looks", cars parked on our lawn, late and noisy basketball games on the driveway next to our house, all became frequent occurrences. Since they knew from a previous request while we were on friendly terms we did not appreciate them leaving their garage lights on all night shining in our bedroom window, those bright lights began to be left on every night to shine in our room. It became an opportunity to get back, and continues to this day. However, with their dysfunctionality, they often leave the lights on all day, and sometimes for several days. Their vindictiveness only hurts them as they waste money while getting even.

For my part, I was more than willing to react toward them

initially, becoming annoyed by everything they did, easily irritated. I have a great "death stare" myself, which I would take every opportunity to use. I would stare effectively, making them uncomfortable when they drove by. Loud comments and demeaning names flew from my mouth, providing insult at every opportunity. I called the second son "Goofy" every chance I could.

I even bought a portable spotlight to shine on their windows, which did get their attention briefly. However, it also provided them with great amusement, leaving me feeling pretty silly for getting so petty. It clearly backfired on me, when I heard them laughing, for they "got me."

Such great fun!, or so I thought at the time. Forget the truths I knew, this is neighbor wars. Of course, neither of us spoke to the other directly. The exception was the youngest daughter, who remained friendly when the conflict first erupted. Passing through our yard to visit a friend as I sat on our deck one summer evening ready to say nothing, she waved and softly said "hello." Did I ever feel foolish! All she cared about was her friendship with me, not the feud that now existed between our families. What a reminder a young girl was smarter than all the rest of us.

I still felt justified being angry with them, and lost no opportunity to judge their actions, whether garbage cans left in the open, junk cars cluttering the driveway, or lights on all night. Yet, I knew different and better. How often, though, do we struggle to live our ideals and values, try to take the higher road, but give into our judgmental, vindictive, vengeful side.

Always we can justify to ourselves the choice to be judgmental and exact retribution. It's especially easy with entitled neighbors when they go out of their way to tell everyone near and far we are the problem, and that we are the ones going out of our way to deliberately harm them. This is particularly easy for them to justify as we were willing to set limits with them which said their behavior could no longer intrude on our space.

The following summer word filtered back to us the woman next door was busily telling everyone around how awful we were treating her. Some neighbors on the street behind us still believe to this day we are the problem neighbors. So it became especially easy for me to be self-righteous since she was lying about us.

Yet I also began to question why this challenge is in my life and how can I respond in a way that resolves this challenge. Certainly escalating with them, responding in kind with vengeance and malice, wasn't the solution. I was even offered a solution involving an organized crime figure, which was momentarily tempting, but not seriously considered. Yet the universe was really giving me a challenge to choose between good and evil, vengeance versus forgiveness.

While it might have been gratifying in the short-term to solve this situation in such a manner, I knew I couldn't live with my own conscience. I also couldn't ignore the reality of universal laws and their consequences. For what goes around does indeed come around.

So, how could I resolve this in an adventurous, positive way? While not easy, solutions were forthcoming from truths I already know and am continually learning.

The first thing I did was visualize a cone of white light surrounding my neighbors and their home. I placed their house in a white light, visualizing, imagining or seeing it there. Problems with them diminished almost immediately! Then I would get irritated with them again, and problems would increase.

I wish I could tell you I readily began the healing process with this challenge, but it isn't always easy to make the right choices, even when we intellectually know it is the better way and know the universe responds positively when we create positively. Emotionally, it seems easier to respond negatively, but the universe also responds in kind to what we create with our thoughts, feelings and mind.

As I write this I can tell you I have become progressively better at meeting this challenge. I am almost to the point now where I have released most negative and fear-based emotions toward them, and provided healing for myself as well. While I still become critical of them at times, I am less focused on what they do wrong, in judging them, and in feeling offended when their dysfunction, entitled behavior recurs.

I use forgiveness affirmations, continue to visualize the

protective, healing light around them, and work to let go of judgment and condemnation. At one point I learned about writing a letter to my angels and their angels, asking for the perfect solution that is for the highest good of all concerned. I wrote the letter, and put it aside as you are supposed to do. As a result even more healing and peace manifested in this situation.

Even with all the positive and love-based actions I practice, there are still times I am hooked by their provocative actions. One such incident occurred during the summer when their guest parked their car over two feet up on our lawn. This was the latest episode of an ongoing problem, despite numerous requests to remove vehicles from our lawn.

The previous Easter a guest of theirs did the same thing. When I politely asked for the vehicle to be moved, the car was reparked off my lawn. Yet later that evening the neighbor's mother and her companion started yelling at us for causing a problem on Easter. When another incident occurred the same summer, we called the police to intervene, which again led to the removal of the vehicle. We were also advised to purchase large rocks to line the edge by the street.

When this next episode happened, I was immediately enraged and pulled my vehicle up against the bumper of the car on my lawn, to send the message that I was offended. This feeling quickly passed and I again felt foolish for reacting in anger from my "human" side. I moved my vehicle, but not before it was noticed I reacted to their latest escapade. To get me back they called the police, who investigated with my cooperation to see if I bumped the vehicle in an assaultive manner.

While the officer initially had an attitude with me, he soon realized he had walked into a situation that was much more complicated. He left and advised the neighbors to have their guests park in front of their house. Unfortunately for me, I again allowed myself to react to their provocations, rather than respond from my own highest good and from my Higher Self. Fortunately, God is not interested in our mistakes, only our solutions. I set about to re-employ the solutions I know work for my higher good and would continue to do so.

As I have done this the conflict melts away. Interestingly, most people don't want to believe me when I tell them these solutions work. Disbelief is evident. The results for me are clear. A positive, loving, forgiving approach does work.

The following autumn I discovered, the morning after a heavy frost, that a car was driven across part of our lawn, killing the grass beneath the protective frost as the tires removed the frost. My psychic friend "saw" the neighbor woman, while apparently intoxicated, driving across the lawn feeling particularly vindictive. By now I was reacting with considerably more calmness.

I continue to send them light, practice forgiveness affirmations, and use other techniques that will allow healing and peace to manifest. Recently I have sent "liquid golden light" from my heart chakra to their heart chakra, asking for their forgiveness and sending my forgiveness.

Liquid golden light is amber in color, and looks like honey being poured from a jar. It is a very healing, cleansing and energizing light. You can visualize, imagine, or feel this light moving all through you, from your feet up through your head. As you try this you may feel a slight tingling sensation as energy pours into you. I am informed by spirit dimension entities this light will even take away all desire for addictive substances, and I have used this successfully with many alcoholics and addicts.

When this light is visualized, and then sent from your heart chakra to another's heart chakra as instructed above, tremendous healing takes place in relationships. Also, considerable resolution of conflict or discord with others takes place as well. I experimented with this one time with a Probate Court judge who seemed particularly unfriendly for no apparent reason. As soon as she entered her courtroom, right after I did this, she immediately looked over to where I was standing, nodded her head in greeting and smiled warmly before she took the bench. Since then she has always been friendly with me.

More recently with my neighbors, I was told to use an affirmation with them in which I call upon my Mighty I AM Presence, the part of God within all of us, to purify their emotional bodies, and fill their emotional bodies with peace.

As these practices are put into action, considerable positive change occurs. I feel more and more at peace, and incidents with them arise very infrequently now. When incidents do arise I now respond calmly. Sometimes I am amazed at how calm I've become. This past summer, despite the rocks which now line the edge of the lawn, tire tracks made by a four-wheel drive vehicle were found early the next morning. My psychic friend confirmed my intuitive feeling the perpetrator of this vandalism was the second son next door, who owns a Jeep Wrangler. This time I responded in a calm, loving manner.

I have since learned this challenge is placed in my life so I can learn many lessons and to resolve karmic debt. Certainly learning how to respond differently with positive and love-based emotions and attitude, applying known universal laws, learning new ways to resolve conflict and create peace have come from this experience. I can almost feel gratitude for the challenge, and believe I will reach that point where I will be truly grateful. I know I will get to the point where I can salute this entitled family for being teachers to me, and feel I am now doing this in a limited way.

Another challenge is being met in an adventurous way. Life is a continuous adventure with many problems and challenges to face. Life gives us endless opportunity to demonstrate truth, to ourselves and others. Since life will give us the same challenge over and over again until we meet it, do something different so the challenge is resolved and the problem goes away. There will be new problems and new challenges, but at least that challenge is gone. I know this challenge is almost over for me. I will continue to strive to see this is so. An adventurous attitude leads me to solutions that work and will lead you to the solutions that work for you as well. Joy will come.

An adventurous attitude helps in meeting life's challenges. I am certainly not thrilled to have this challenge in my life. To buy a dream house and end up with entitled neighbors next door has been very trying. Yet, with an adventurous attitude this challenge becomes a wonderful opportunity to learn, to grow, and to ultimately learn about love, among many other lessons.

Recently I am now able to see my neighbors in the healing light of love, and to behold the truth of their being at the spiritual level, behind the facade of their entitled behavior. I can see the Christ in them, free of my own judgments and ill feelings toward their surface behaviors. Indeed, a monumental challenge has become a real opportunity, helping me to put into action basic truths. As I apply these truths I create joy for myself. You too can face your challenges and adversities, apply universal laws, and create your joy.

CHAPTER NINE

HOW TO CREATE REAL MAGIC IN OUR LIVES

Our thoughts create our reality. The way we think produces the very world in which we live. If we have thoughts of joy, prosperity and abundance, positive and loving relationships, numerous and meaningful friendships, and peace in our daily lives, then these will manifest for us. If, instead, we have thoughts of unhappiness, lack, and failure, negative and fearful relationships, little or no friends, and conflict and hate in our daily lives, then these too will be present.

One of the changes I made, to resolve conflict with my entitled neighbors, was to change my mind about them. As I shifted my attitude from condemnation and negativity to at least neutrality, while employing positive approaches, and working toward loving acceptance, then dramatic changes occurred in the level of conflict with them. Shift in attitude is the product of a change in thinking.

Edgar Cayce constantly reminded us in the psychic readings he gave that "mind is the builder." What we think about and how we think about everything shapes the world we live in. Norman Vincent Peale wrote extensively about the benefits of positive thought. He continually reminded us of the power of positive thinking. Napoleon Hill discovered in studying highly successful people that what the mind can conceive, and believe, it will achieve.

Adventurous living is understanding the power of the mind, and applying this power in a positive way each day of our lives. It is also about imagining the highest fantasy we can have for ourselves, so we can create this in our lives and manifest the path of joy. By highest, I am referring here to the fantasy which best serves our mission and purpose through our partnership with God.

All reality in our life, whether at the physical, mental, emotional or spiritual level, is created through the manifestation of thought. Remember, the power of thought is such that when our Creator began creation, He uttered "the word" which in the beginning brought this universe into existence. The Archangel Metatron shared in a reading with me that with one word God created the world. God gave us the very same gift, the capacity to create with our thoughts.

While we may not be able to create planets, we can create the kind of world we want to live in. Together, with our thoughts, we certainly can create the collective world we live in. A world of peace, harmony and abundance awaits us, if together, we choose to create it with thoughts of peace, harmony and abundance.

Each of us create our lives with our thoughts. Edgar Cayce frequently reminded us the physical is the result of the thoughts we have. Even physical illness manifests according to our thoughts. Increasingly we are coming to understand how our thoughts and attitude contribute to becoming ill, how the illness will manifest, and how the healing process will progress. Louise Hay, among others, has studied the psychological and emotional components of various maladies.

While many of our physicians still don't entirely believe in the mind-body connection, it is increasingly clear that stress and the emotional state of the person contribute to the course of an illness, as well as the course of the healing process. Behind stress and our emotional states are the thoughts and choices which bring these states into existence within us.

If our thoughts do indeed create our reality, it is important to recognize the tremendous potential which exists through the power of our minds. Deepak Chopra has written the mind transcends the physical body, and seems to envelop it. He further states intelligence exists within each and every cell of the body. If mind transcends the physical brain, and this mental body is linked to Superconscious Mind or Universal Mind, then possibility thinking gives us the opportunity to manifest better choices. Adventurous living is becoming a possibility thinker.

How to create possibility thinking in our lives requires moving beyond the belief in lack and limitation. For most of humanity the predominate belief system is lack. Believing this, we experience lack and limitation. Then, with circular reasoning, we say to ourselves there is not enough to go around. The belief in lack extends to every area of life. We come to believe in and accept lack even within ourselves. We become critical of others and ourselves, and we begin to accept there is not enough, within and without ourselves.

This belief in lack extends to self-love and self-worth. Through the disappointments and failures we experience, as well as the critical comments of significant people in our lives, we come to believe we lack in talent, ability, competence, and the ability to learn new things.

For years I held the belief I lacked the ability to build things and work with my hands. In spite of this I decided to undertake a significant building project, building a trellis to shade a deck area. Because of my belief in lack I approached this project with much fear, but I was determined to overcome this fear and lack of self-confidence to succeed with carpentry and a construction project. Suddenly, I discovered with patience, trial and error, and reading instructions as I went along, I could build a complicated trellis enclosing a large deck area. I finished with a beautiful addition that was a finishing touch to what became a lovely area. No longer did I believe in a lack of ability in this area.

Lack extends to many areas. Most of us believe there is not enough prosperity, not only for us, but for most of the world. Included in this is a belief that we lack resources, that the world has limits in its capacity to allow us to live with abundance and comfort.

Lack extends to families and relationships, to work and career, to almost every area we can think of. Often the excuse is made that if only we had the right situation, people or circumstances in our lives, then all should be well, and happiness and contentment will result. Yet the belief in lack creates the very lack that perpetuates the beliefs we operate by and manifest with.

Limitation particularly arises when we solely operate with our rational mind, disregarding the other half which is intuitive, creative, and artistic in it's functioning. Further, I would suggest to you we only use about 10% of our brain's capacity. As we expand and move into greater mind and it's endless potential, transformation becomes possible as we create with greater understanding and wisdom. Superconsciousness awaits as we move forward from the limitations of the intellectual, and as we move forward into "knowing" and all possibilities. Our attitude shifts as we move from restricted thought, lack and limitation into possibility thinking.

We make choices by how we think. If we engage in denial, minimization and avoidance of pain, and victimization, we will create with thoughts filled with doubt and fear. Doubt and fear interfere with the power of positive thinking. When we are busy being offended by everything, our egos reign supreme, and daily awareness is just about survival. We manifest limitation and lack in our lives with restricted awareness.

When we banish doubt, when we are willing to suspend disbelief, then increased awareness results. We can have higher levels of awareness in our relationships. We can create prosperity and abundance. We can heal ourselves and stay healthy without relying on drugs to do so. We can eliminate addictions and dependencies. Nothing is impossible. The Apostle Mark wrote, "To he that believeth, all things are possible." We can choose to release all negative and limiting beliefs, and accept the unlimited potential greater awareness and wisdom provide us.

As we gain in greater understanding and awareness, we then access divine mind, superconsciousness, or master mind. A knowingness arises in our thinking, which is the consciousness which sees that all things are possible. Real magic is created by our thoughts with this awareness.

As we begin to believe in possibility, we move forward in expanded awareness now creating and manifesting all possibility. Ever expanding success and potential await us. If there are no limits, if there are endless possibilities, combined with the belief that all is possible and can be manifested, the results will be wonderful. Many successful athletes do this all the time, visualizing the success, believing in their ability to manifest that success, with results naturally flowing from their visualization.

Thoughts are powerful. They create the world we live in, individually and collectively. Since thoughts are powerful, control of the mind is essential, if we are going to live peacefully, joyfully, and healthfully. We need to train the mind always to be loving and kind, and to see the best in others and in everything. What we give our love, time, and attention to, we get more of. We must become aware of our thoughts, for our thoughts determine our experiences.

We have the freedom to accept and embrace whatever thoughts we choose. We possess the ability to think, create and become whatever we want to become. It is necessary to take our thoughts off the negative and fear-based and think only about those things we want to be part of our life. Our lives reflect our thoughts, dreams, expectations, beliefs, hopes, feelings of self-worth and desires. Knowing this we can consciously modify our inner states to create and live our highest potential and vision.

We are not victims of circumstance, for there are no coincidences. Further, since we create our reality by our thoughts, the world about us reflects what we are focusing our thoughts on. We are the architects of our lives. Our conscious thoughts create the image of our lives, ourselves, and our feelings. We create our own heaven or hell by the choices in thought and attitude we make. Our thoughts can imprison or set us free. Adversities, challenges and painful realities do not upset us, but the way we think about them does.

When we take charge of ourselves, of our thoughts, emotions, words and actions, all things respond. As we accept the free will God has given us, and through the activity of our connection with divine mind, we have the power to retrain our minds and be in control. No matter how long or often we have misused our minds, we can still use our minds in ways which are positive and for our greatest good.

Negative thoughts bring negative results. We attract back what we express and think. As noted earlier, what we think as well as what we do returns to us tenfold. If you want joy and happiness, begin to visualize and affirm these in your life. As we become consciously aware of our thinking, we change the patterns in our lives, allowing the positive and good to emerge. Focus your thoughts on what you want for yourself and the world. When we focus on positive thoughts we feel empowered and good, radiating positive energy which attracts what we want in our lives. Jesus said this simply, "As you think, so shall you be."

As stated earlier, what we can conceive, and believe, we can achieve. Key to this is the use of our imagination. The imagery we use to envision our dreams, goals, desires, and hopes is the key to self mastery. Conscious, creative visualization is one tool for using our imagination, practiced with feeling, thanksgiving, and acceptance. Visualizing goals becomes an important way we manifest what we want in our lives through the power of the mind.

Jack Boland taught the principle of Master Minding as a way to conceive, believe and achieve. Calling upon the Master Mind that exists within each of us, we can move beyond limitation and lack to possibility and abundance. He developed a transforming system of thought that became a guide, an organizing system, to use imagination and affirmation to manifest this Master Mind consciousness. This system includes four components: the use of a yearly journal to develop and review goals; developing a year long contract with our Higher Power to ask what we want in our lives as well as what we will give back; a guide on how to create an image book to further visualize our goals; and, working with others to collectively visualize and achieve goals.

The Master Mind Journal is set up to help one identify yearly, monthly, and weekly goals. Used daily one reminds him/herself of goals established, progress toward goals, and daily journaling on successes and blessings in their lives.

An important part of the Master Mind process is writing a contract that affirms our partnership with God on a yearly basis, involving both what we would like to receive as well as what we will give in return. This guides our imagination in conceiving what we would like to achieve, as well as affirming our belief that our partnership with God will manifest all that we conceive. Equally important, this contract calls upon us to give back to the universe, cementing our partnership with God, and allowing Co-Creation to occur.

The Master Mind process also involves creating an image book. This is accomplished by creating visual images to support the goals we wish to achieve. Words and pictures are cut out from magazines and other sources, as well as making use of drawings, to create the visions of what we want to manifest in our lives and in the world. Looking at these images on a daily basis helps Master Mind consciousness to emerge, bringing about achievement of these visions.

Finally, the Master Mind process involves having a partner or partners to allow the collective mind and support to bring goals into reality. It is both a visualization process and an affirmation process as the group supports each members goals, hopes and dreams. The consciousness of the entire group accelerates the belief process, achieving the concepts each person desires to manifest.

Belief in what we can achieve is enhanced with enthusiasm. Enthusiasm is a God-given quality that we must choose to bring to whatever we think and do. When we call for enthusiasm, we can meet all challenges and meet life with faith. When we act out with enthusiasm, when we become it, what we are thinking manifests in an accelerated manner. The attitude of enthusiasm becomes an affirmation in and of itself. It says what we expect and believe will come into being. Thinking creates results, and enthusiasm generates the change that brings achievement and reality to all we believe.

We can choose to celebrate life, live life fully, and make a positive difference. Health, happiness, peace, abundance, and success are choices. Living our vision gives us the power to achieve our goals. Susan Smith Jones states, "All you have ever dreamed, thought, or needed in your life has contributed to what you have at this very moment. So if things aren't just the way you would like them to be, and you want to change them, you must change your thoughts and the words you speak to express those thoughts."

From this moment on, choose consciously to take your attention off things that you don't want in your life, and think about and visualize what you do want. The key is to see and experience only the way you would like life to be for you. Let your vision for yourself be successful and positive, and let it be the highest fantasy you can create for yourself.

Verbal affirmations of what we want to accomplish or the reality we want to create for ourself can supplement our positive thoughts. During the day, affirm to yourself a statement that will bring about the positive results you want. Your affirmations should always be in the positive, present and successful state. If you are stating things in the future tense, they will not become a reality. For example, say "I am," not "I will be." Never allow anyone or anything to cause you to doubt your power and ability to live your vision-to manifest your goals and dreams.

Goals are an important part of creating our vision, of creating the highest fantasy we can have for our life. They give us something constructive to think about. Goals give our thoughts positive direction and purpose. Let imagination work. Know that you are exactly where you need to be in life and, at any moment, you can choose to experience something else by simply taking responsibility and consciously choosing to think differently.

Les Brown writes, "Decide consciously to develop a loving spirit about life, starting now, just being very loving. Experience that. Get up, with an attitude of gratitude, first thing in the morning, with a smile on your face. When you have this kind of attitude, you walk with a different kind of beat. When you have that kind of energy, that kind of consciousness, people will enjoy being around you. You feel better physically. You move with a little more sparkle. Just try it out...see what happens."

He reminds us that the right attitude, created with our own thoughts, leads to a different focus. This new focus is on the power of the mind to create what we believe, and to make choices reflecting the higher good we want to manifest in our lives. We have the choice about the attitudes we want to live by, the vision we want to create, the kind of world we want to live in.

Gloria Swenders has written the following poem, "Choices," which sums up the power of the mind. It goes like this:

Emotions are created within ourselves.
We have a "choice" for happiness or sorrow,
Decisions on how we perform and react,
If someone upsets or troubles us,
We should say "God bless their soul."
Influence and empowerment are important factors,
We must keep our mind in control.
We always bless the good in people,
But forget to bless the bad. In
our sudden confusion or anger

We forget the choice we had.
The people who seem to be at low,
Need our blessings most of all.
Ask that peace be with them,
Let the trinity stand tall.
We all have confrontations
And each has a story to tell.
When you find your self content,
Then you've made your choices well."

    The title of this chapter is borrowed from Wayne Dyer, who states that inside our physical being is divine organizing intelligence. Different levels of awareness go along with this divine organizing intelligence. Dyer writes there are high, higher, and highest levels of awareness beyond the awareness of simple survival. When we contact these higher levels we can create anything in our lives. We can create miracles. This is what Jesus meant when he said "Even the least among you can do all that I have done and even greater things." We all have the same organizing intelligence.

    Thoughts literally create circumstances. Knowing this we need to be cautious about what our thoughts are focused on. They create our reality, and it comes to us tenfold.

    In working with many of my clients, I teach them to use affirmations, which demonstrates this process or reality. Whether an affirmation for better employment, or for the right relationship, or for whatever is needed in their lives right now, I have them use this process to achieve their goals. Affirmations are commands to the universe to provide us what we need and want. It is important to request this, asking for what will help us that is for our highest good.

    We can manifest real magic in our lives as we gain in awareness, and create with higher level thoughts. Adventurous living requires choices on how we think. Why not create real magic in your life using principles of mind to create the reality you want to live in, as well as create the world we all live in. As we use mind in a positive, enthusiastic way, we create a new reality. Goals and imagination come into existence as we visualize and affirm what we want our lives and our world to be. As we expand our awareness, as our consciousness grows, we begin to experience the positive choices of our new thoughts.

Understanding the power of thought, the importance of the power of positive thinking, we can use our minds in a more positive way to create the vision of our life we wish to manifest for ourselves. Create the highest fantasy for yourself, using visualization and affirmation to bring these into being.

CHAPTER TEN

GRATITUDE

Right thought, creative thought, begins by developing the right attitude. Right attitude begins by having an attitude of gratitude. Adventurous living is learning to appreciate and to be grateful for everything in our lives. Applying this attitude helps us to manifest the path of joy in life on a continual basis.

Gratitude is a joyful celebration of thanksgiving for all that is experienced, as well as for all we have, from the smallest to the greatest. It is being thankful for all that is, all that was, and all that will be. It becomes a way of thinking. Putting it into practice facilitates the path of spiritual discovery while creating our lives as masterpieces of joy. When practiced on a daily basis, a true appreciation of life and all it has to offer emerges for us. Awareness of life itself becomes magnified as gratitude is made a regular practice on a daily basis.

When depressed and anxious clients come to me, the first thing I do is assign them to walk daily from 20 to 30 minutes. I instruct them to follow this no matter what the season, for it is important to do this year round.

While the walking itself is beneficial, as it stimulates endorphin production in the brain which leads to brighter mood and calmer coping with stressors, a larger purpose is at work as well. Often when walking we become aware of nature and its rhythms and cycles, even in the midst of the city. We become aware of seasonal changes and the subtle moods of seasons as they progress. We become reacquainted with the rhythms of this planet we live on.

We see again the subtle fabric of life as well as the overall beauty of nature. We begin to appreciate once again the beauty of the world we live in. Living in an advanced technological society we are divorced from the planet which nurtures us. With modern forms of transportation, heaters and air conditioners which protect us from the range of temperature about us, and with many forms of electronic media to occupy our minds and our time, we are disconnected from

Mother Earth who nourishes us physically, mentally, emotionally and spiritually. No wonder so many of us are stressed out, depressed and anxious.

Connecting again with the rhythm and flow of life allows us to reconnect with all life. We reconnect to the physical structure of ourselves which is intimately connected to the pulse of life on this planet. Daily walks do reconnect us, and in doing so, we begin to experience again an attitude of gratitude, for this naturally flows from feeling connected to nature and to the planet.

Even relationships are enhanced when we walk daily with our loved ones and our friends. Children naturally enjoy being connected with parents on daily excursions. Even our dogs eagerly partake of these daily walks, connecting to us and to the world about them.

The process of appreciation for nature reminds us of the process of gratitude. As appreciation arises within, we become grateful for the rich fabric of life sustained on this planet. Appreciation then moves forward to a more active process of practicing gratitude for all that is.

I moved back to the Midwest from California during October 1978. Since Autumn is a favorite season for me anyway, the five years I lived in California I missed this season tremendously. One year the mother of a group home resident I worked with visited the Midwest. She brought back a bag full of multicolored leaves for me. Her small token was greatly appreciated as I again beheld the wonder of nature in its Autumn array.

So when I drove across the United States that Fall I was completely enthralled and in ecstasy the entire journey. I delighted in the changes of color in the trees as I beheld their full glory. Whether the sparse trees lining river beds in the West, with bold swatches of color streaked across them, or the forests of Eastern Oklahoma and Missouri, or the woods of the Midwest, I often shouted out loud in joy and the beauty before me. No doubt others passing me by wondered if I was crazy or high on something. I was naturally high at re-experiencing the full wonder of Autumn once again. I didn't care what anyone else thought, for I was in gratitude for the awesome display nature gives us in the Fall.

Gratitude is an attitude and a way of thinking which can be applied on a daily basis. While it is easy to start with nature on daily walks, we can learn to implement it and practice it in all things.

Start with abundance and prosperity. Express gratitude for what you already have, and do this every day. Eliminate the idea of lack in life. See what is there and acknowledge all you have with gratitude. See more abundance and prosperity coming, and express thankfulness for what will be coming. Each day thank God for the abundant gifts He has bestowed on you and your family, and for those yet to come.

Michael Wickett, motivational speaker, shared how this process began to work for him as he began to learn about prosperity consciousness. He was at his lowest financially, with a meager and poorly furnished apartment, few belongings or clothes, and a rusted, old car.

He began consciously expressing gratitude for what he did have, focusing on the positive, rather than on lack. He began feeling gratitude for his rusted, old car for at least it got him where he needed to go. It helped him work toward his long-term goals to succeed in motivational speaking by getting to the audiences who needed to hear what he had to say. He expressed gratitude for having a place to live, shelter from the elements, and enough belongings to get by and to survive with some comfort. His focus in a positive direction, rather than on lack, opened his mind to possibility thinking. It also created his partnership with God which opened doors of opportunity, and helped him to succeed in his chosen endeavor. Gratitude also helped him to overcome any thoughts of limitation, so he could move forward with his vision and create his dream. Prosperity and abundance naturally followed.

Too often we look at what we don't have, the perceived lack in our life. For instance, we accept the idea abundance is only measured in financial terms, missing the very abundance we do have in many areas. Living through a very prosperous period in the history of the world, we focus on what advertisers convince us we must have to be happy, so we begin to experience lack instead of appreciation for what we do have. Gratitude begins with recognizing and appreciating what we do have, accepting all "gifts" with humility and thankfulness.

Gratitude begins with the basics, such as having a roof over our heads, food to eat at each meal, and other basic necessities. It is also thankfulness for having the means to provide these things. Many express their gratitude by simply praying with thanksgiving before each meal. By simply thanking God, and then the animal and plant kingdoms for their contributions to our health and well-being, we quicken the molecular structure of the food and enhance the nutrients which bless us. Native Americans and other indigenous peoples have long known and practiced this.

What many call primitive people best understand how thanking nature and each kingdom for the sustenance provided activates spiritual principles which improve what is being received. Learning to consciously thank Earth Mother and The Source enhance the benefits to us. Further, we signal to the universe our gratitude and assure a continual flow of good into our lives. Gratitude for the simple things opens up the possibility for even greater abundance and good in our lives.

Money is one way prosperity is measured in our society. Gratitude for the money received keeps the flow of abundance going. Each time I receive and deposit money I say a prayer of thanksgiving. Each time I pay a bill or send money out I thank God for the abundance in my life so I can pay those bills.

Even checks paid for taxes are sent with love and gratitude, and a request they are of assistance for the good government does provide. I visualize my contribution going to the positive things government does with the money. Jack Boland shared the idea sending out money, even to the IRS, with joy and gratitude created more prosperity and abundance.

Money is only the root of all evil if the attitude in which it is sent or received is evil. If greed, control and power are the purpose of money for you then it will be evil. In truth, money is neither good nor evil. It is the thought connected to money that determines the outcome.

Prosperity and abundance go far beyond material wealth, a distinction often lost in our materialistic society. More and better toys don't make us happy. People often respond to this by saying they wouldn't mind still being miserable, at least they would be rich. But being rich doesn't make us happy. If it did, everyone who lives in a wealthy community would be very happy. Guess what? They're not.

Financial worry and fear can certainly be stressors. However, material gain in and of itself won't bring happiness. There are many people who can't get enough, as they desperately try to fill the emptiness deep within themselves. True prosperity and abundance can include many material things, but it is the richness of life itself that is true prosperity and abundance.

Anyone who experiences a serious health challenge suddenly finds the things they once thought were important no longer matter. To be healthy and free from physical suffering and handicaps are a great gift to have. It is important to be grateful for good health. Expressing this gratefulness on a daily basis is paramount.

Honor the physical body and the marvelous way it works, for it allows us to experience the physical dimensions. The body truly is a temple of the Living God. Honor and gratitude for this temple is appropriate. Being grateful also extends to taking good care of ourselves by eating right, exercising regularly, and not abusing our bodies.

Gratitude extends to our families and loved ones. This includes parents, siblings, spouses, children and other relatives. It may extend to an adopted family as well, if we needed to find others to replace dysfunctional and toxic members of our own family. It is sometimes useful to do this to survive and grow emotionally.

When we have toxic family members it may be very difficult to find anything about them to be grateful for. Don't deny the dysfunctional or toxic qualities in that person, but also try to find something about them you can be grateful for. Perhaps there was something they said or did which was positive and was helpful to you or to others. Gratitude may only be that a dysfunctional or toxic person provided you with the "right" or "necessary" experiences you needed to become who you are now.

Express and feel gratitude for friends. In friends and acquaintances, coworkers and colleagues are important relationships.

Feel gratitude for these friends and associates, recognizing the valuable contributions these relationships give to us.

Recognize and honor the work you do, the role you play, the career you have. Too often employment is seen as just a job, with begrudging acceptance or a focus on what is wrong at work rather than on what is right about it. Recognize and honor the work you do, the role you play, the career you have. Recognize the best in the job or career path, and allow gratitude for what the job allows you to be or do. Sometimes the value is simply as a source of income which gives the freedom to pursue other interests or passions which aren't financially rewarded.

I've consulted at one hospital for four years. Many of the tasks I have there are dull and routine, and certainly not as exciting or invigorating as some of the work I do in private sessions with clients or in the supervisory work I do with clinicians. Yet this role provides me with dependable and regular income which allows me the opportunity to do the other work I enjoy.

I also have wonderful friends and acquaintances at that hospital. I have a mission and purpose there as well, which often transcends the defined role, especially when I share spiritual awareness and truth with some, or affirm and enjoy basic truths with others as we share experiences together. Every time I wonder why I'm still there, something new happens which affirms my part in the divine plan as it unfolds and operates. At times, there are simply events I'm to experience before I move on.

Even unpleasant events and experiences are there to give me an opportunity to practice and apply fundamental truths, so we can learn and continue to increase in awareness. There is much to be grateful for, whether continued supply, wonderful relationships, challenging relationships, the opportunity to be of service, or the chances to continue growing, even with unpleasantness.

Experience gratitude for life itself, and this marvelous planet we live on. Honor your own life in the physical, and the wonderful, diverse interplay of life on this planet. Gratitude for the blessings of life, and thankfulness for being alive in this realm give honor for the greatest gift we have from a loving Creator at this moment in time and space.

Gratitude to all of life creates harmony with all living things, and with Mother Earth herself who is also a living, sentient being. All creation has consciousness at some level, so as we express our thanks and appreciation to all things we honor that which in turn sustains us. Indigenous peoples understand this principle well. They attempt to live in harmony and express appreciation to all of life, to the forces and elements of nature, to the elemental and devic kingdoms, to the energy of the sun, and to the planet herself.

Our separation from the rest of life, and our belief dominion means exploitation, has led to the technological and ecological crises we face. Dominion actually means stewardship, being guardians of the planet. Healing these crises we face means working together in collective consciousness, expressing gratefulness for all of life, and gratefulness for the interconnectedness which ultimately makes life more harmonious and joyful. For we are all one. We are a collective whole on this spinning orb in the vast cosmos. We are also one with the cosmos.

Each person's spiritual heritage is a wonderful place to express gratitude, since we are spiritual beings having a human experience. Honoring ourselves not in the physical sense but in the spiritual sense. Our spiritual heritage is a key element in this process of gratitude, for we are indeed made in the image and likeness of God. As we learn to reconnect to our spiritual heritage, and listen and attend to our higher self within, life begins to flow more smoothly with greater meaning and purpose in all we do. The higher self is the direct link each person has with God.

Gratitude for this personal relationship each of us has with God, the capacity to know God is in each and everyone, as well as is all things, and the connection each of us has with God is an important way we honor the Creator and our own divinity. Each of us has the "still, small voice within" available to know the will of God in our life. Gratitude enhances this connection, and enhances the recognition of our partnership with God.

Each person's spiritual heritage includes the hierarchy of beings beneath God who stand by to assist. To know and to express gratitude to these beings aids spiritual growth and development as well as aiding successful and joyful living. Each one of us has spiritual guides, sometimes referred to as guardian angels. These are discarnate beings who stand by to assist, influence and guide. We are in touch with these beings through dreams, intuition and direct knowing when we consciously allow communication to flow with them. In the regression hypnosis and the vision hypnosis I do with clients, these guides have come forth to offer understanding and assistance. As always, we express our appreciation for their ongoing aid.

Other higher dimensional beings stand by to assist us as needed. Through the vision hypnosis process, angels, archangels and ascended masters have been frequent visitors, providing understanding and assistance as needed. In a vision hypnosis session recently the client's abusive mother, now deceased, came to her during the session and attempted to be manipulative and harmful with her once again, this time from spirit realms. The Archangel Michael came to her aid, assisting us in commanding the mother to leave and to never return. Archangel Michael has come on other occasions for this client, providing information, instruction and protection. Thus, it wasn't surprising when he came again to be of help.

During vision hypnosis sessions many higher dimensional beings have come to provide assistance, instruction and healing. Distinguished "visitors" have included the ascended master Lord Sanada, who we know as Jesus; the ascended master St. Germain; Merlin, who is the historian for this universe; and, recently the Buddha. All have provided loving guidance and support to clients as they deal with the issues before them. They also indicate they are available at any time if we just call upon them for assistance and guidance. Remember, Jesus promised us if we called he would always come.

Our cosmic brothers and sisters also warrant our gratitude, for many of them have been assisting humanity for centuries, insuring we don't destroy ourselves and the planet while we struggle to remember our divine heritage and manifest it in our lives on a continual basis. They have stood by, keeping the planet intact, working with the planetary energy grids which keep this orb together physically. They are serving us so the peaceful unfoldment of the divine plan for this planet can be achieved. Although many don't want to acknowledge the possibility extraterrestrial life may exist, our cosmic brothers have faithfully aided us.

Whether angels, cosmic beings, or other higher dimensional beings, we can experience communication with them. They stand by to aid, communicate, guide and assist. Gratitude for their aid is important, and allows lines of communication to remain open and accessible.

Oftentimes, various life experiences and lessons provide valuable opportunities for learning, growth and increased awareness. As previously discussed, life offers many lessons, even with adversities, challenges and painful realities. Pain does diminish with time, and we can choose to let go of pain at any time and with time. Holding on to guilt, blame and shame doesn't facilitate growth. Emotionally beating up on ourselves doesn't lead to meaningful or positive change. Learning from the experiences, understanding what took place so we can make better choices the next time, and the ability to master subsequent situations are the beneficial outcomes of all learning experiences, pleasant or unpleasant.

Learning opportunities become another place where gratitude can be chosen. Learning to be thankful and appreciative for life experiences which facilitate growth further enhances awareness and increases self-worth. This can be as simple as brief acknowledgement of thanks for all situations and experiences which help us achieve greater wisdom and awareness of universal truths.

More challenging is feeling gratitude for adversity and failure. More and more these days the message is life should be free from failure. Life is always supposed to flow smoothly, with no adversity to hold one back, nor failure to mar self-esteem. Yet adversity and failure are absolutely essential features of life. With no challenges to face and to master, we have little or no opportunity to learn, grow and gain in wisdom and understanding.

Failure is filled with negative connotations that don't need to be there. While no one likes to experience failure, it will occur in most areas of life at one time or another. Who hasn't failed at a friendship, a love, a relationship, a job, an educational endeavor or reaching a goal? You can play it safe, never risking or trying, but greater achievement and ultimately happiness elude those who don't attempt to meet life's challenges. Even in times of adversity and failure we progress. Self-love and self-worth are ultimately better when we risk, when we try, when we dare to meet and greet all challenges.

Adversaries can also become our greatest source of learning and growth. Adversaries provide us with immediate challenges to live and manifest spiritual truths, just as my entitled neighbors provide for me. Enemies give us the chance to practice spiritual truth as taught by all the master teachers throughout history. We especially get to practice love and forgiveness. Adversaries and enemies come into our lives to provide us with whatever lesson we need to learn. If you have an enemy, figure out what the lesson is you are meant to learn.

The universe has a wonderful capacity to provide us with the experience we need, over and over again, until we learn the lesson. While I haven't been overly thrilled or excited about my entitled neighbors, and have struggled at times to manifest spiritual truth with them, I know they're in my life for a reason. They provide me with innumerable opportunities to practice a positive, loving, forgiving approach, to recognize and overcome lingering resentments, judgments, vindictiveness and anger.

Enemies give us the opportunity to accept where others are, even as we disagree with them and their choices. They are doing the best they can with what they know at the time. They can be severely limited by their awareness, but this may be where they are. From my awareness I can choose to respond differently and not to judge at all. I can work to behold their true spiritual nature, the Christ within, beyond outward appearances and behavior. Their outward appearances are the product of their egos, just as my outward appearances may at times be the result of my own ego.

The limitations created by others' egos also serve as mirrors to us. We can then recognize and perceive our own faults and errors which can then be corrected. It is easy to project fault and condemnation onto others. Jesus warned us about finding the sliver in another's eye missing the log in our own.

The choice is to accept gratitude for our adversaries and enemies, for they too provide us with a chance to learn about ourselves, to learn discernment about others, and to manifest spiritual truths in difficult situations, not just when it is easy. Letting go of anger, resentment and judgment are rich and rewarding experiences we can be truly grateful for.

Finally, it is important not only to recognize and experience gratitude, it is equally important to express and share gratitude whenever possible and appropriate. This begins with expressing gratitude and thanksgiving to the marvelous Creator from whom all good things flow. Starting with God, openly express appreciation and thanks. The Lord's prayer begins with gratitude, "hallowed by thy Name." Thank God for all the gifts received each day.

Express gratitude often with loved ones, sharing with them how you feel. Thank them for all they do, and for helping to make your life complete, enriched and rewarding. Let co-workers, colleagues and friends know how grateful you are for having them in your life and helping you along the way. Share with your parents your appreciation for what they provided and taught you. Honor them for bringing you into the world. Focus on the positive, even when the dysfunctional and negative also were present to bless you along the way. Share with your children the joy they bring to your life.

Let others know when they've added to your life. Let grateful thoughts be directed to all areas of your life which contribute to your well-being and sustain you. Thank all the animal, elemental and devic kingdoms, this planet and this universe. Allow gratitude to come forth and share it when and where you can.

Gratitude is an attitude. It is a way of thinking, a way of relating to others, to life and all the experiences of life. Joyful living, prosperity and abundance in all areas, and self-love and self-worth readily emerge when possibility thinking includes an attitude of gratitude. Getting into the habit of thinking with appreciation and thankfulness, then sharing this whenever possible, creates the path of joy.

CHAPTER ELEVEN

LOVE

Part of adventurous living is experiencing and giving love. Not just falling in love at least once in life, but experiencing and expressing love in all its many ways and forms. Ultimately, adventurous living is learning to experience and express universal love—an at-one-ness with all-that-is. The application of giving and receiving love is essential to manifesting joy in our lives.

There is a wonderful line in the movie "Ghost" when the character played by Patrick Swayze is finally ready to go into the light, leaving his wife behind. Able to make contact with her directly, he tells her what he has learned. He says to her, "It's amazing Molly, the love you have inside, you take it with you." This summarizes an ultimate truth of this planet, all you take when you leave is the love you give and receive. While I believe you also take the wisdom and the knowing you gain in a physical incarnation when you transition to other realms, a wonderful truth is nonetheless expressed in that movie. It is the capacity to love and be loved which is the greatest gift to give and to receive in life.

Certainly to be in love for the first time, or any subsequent time, is a wonderful and exhilarating experience. To be awash in romantic love, to be light-hearted and carefree, focused on the beauty and wonder of that other person, is a grand experience. The magical feeling of falling in love and being in love combines the freshness of Spring, the pleasure and joy of any special holiday, and the wonder of nature all combined into one glorious moment in time. If we are fortunate, we never stop being in love with a special someone for a very long time or even a lifetime.

Yet, as special as romantic love is, it pales in comparison to the deep and abiding love that evolves between two people when they commit to their relationship. In that commitment, together they face the challenges and obstacles that can easily lead to failure instead of success. For the essence of love in a long-term, committed relationship, is to face all challenges together, overcoming the obstacles that can destroy rather than build. To create a relationship in which there is mutual sharing, problem solving, and decision making is hard work.

Living happily ever after only comes through the effort to make a relationship work, to move beyond manipulative patterns to authentic and genuine risk-taking, relating and vulnerability. In the process of giving needed to create and continually renew a relationship, a depth of love and sharing emerges which is almost beyond words to describe. A truly deep and abiding love comes to exist between two people.

As glorious and wonderful as love can be with a special person, other forms, variations or varieties of love are no less important or meaningful to adventurous living. For love is one of two basic emotions. The other basic emotion is fear. All other emotions have at their core one of these two basic emotions. A Course in Miracles simply states that what is not of love is of fear. Ultimately, love is letting go of fear.

In my therapeutic work with clients, the core work is helping people to release negative and fear-based emotions, replacing them with love, light, peace and forgiveness. Whether through hypnosis or more traditional therapy approaches, the client is lead to discover the root cause which is the source from which the issues and problems they struggle with stem from.

In particular, with regression hypnosis and vision hypnosis, the subconscious mind takes them to the memory which is most in need of healing. The person's subconscious mind always leads them to the memory or experience they can safely handle at that moment in time. Someone who doesn't believe in past lives won't go there until they're ready to accept this possibility. Someone fearful about the larger love and wisdom of the universe won't experience that possibility until sufficient fear is released so the experience will be positive, and not create any more guilt, blame or shame.

When the source of the powerful or sometimes traumatic event is recalled, I instruct the person to release the negative and fear-based emotions into the light, and replace them with healing light and energy. Always, this healing light and energy include love, as well as peace, forgiveness and other positive and love-based emotions.

As noted earlier, with vision hypnosis protocols the right vision, experience or entity emerges which will best help facilitate understanding and awareness. Sometimes higher dimensional beings come forward. At other times the client progresses to a future vision or probability in their life. Some have experienced the angelic realms. Two clients have witnessed creation, one being the birth of a universe.

The person who witnessed the birth of a universe, watched the event unfold with tears of joy streaming down her cheeks, understanding she is part of a vast and grand creative process, not limited by seeming worries and everyday cares. One individual even experienced traveling to the Great Central Sun, experiencing joy and ecstasy as he touched the face of God. In one special moment he experienced the complete depth and eternal splendor of Love that is our Creator.

Part of the purpose of this third dimensional experience is to understand and transcend fear, so we can truly know love. Each letter of the word fear stands for a four word description of what fear is. Fear is False Expectations Appearing Real.

All negative and destructive emotions have at their core the emotion of fear. Whether anger, hate, resentment or jealousy, fear is at the core. Take jealousy and possessiveness for example. The individual fears their loved one will abandon or betray them. As a result they try to control the outcome through possessive and jealous behaviors, manipulating and controlling the other person to guarantee they won't leave.

The paradox here is the more they try to control the other person, the more they drive them away. For no one can flourish in their own autonomy, so they are free to return love fully and completely, if they are manipulated and controlled by another. If the person isn't driven away, they become defeated, submissive and compliant such that the very love so desperately wanted by the controlling person is no more available to them.

The false expectations appearing real are that love should be risk-free, that relationships should always succeed, that the other can't be depended upon to love them back, that one can't live without the other, and that happiness can only come when another is under their control. We can never lose love, even when we lose a particular relationship or loved one. Since our happiness isn't dependent on any person or thing, there are always abundant others available to give and receive love with.

There is always another person available to love and be loved. There are always abundant others and things that fill our world when we radiate with love from within. The truth is if you want love, be loving. Be loving of yourself and all others. Give the love we bask in eternally from our Creator.

Fear, those false expectations appearing real, has created most of the misery and suffering this world has known and continues to know. Belief in victimhood is one of the most destructive forms of fear. It certainly is one of the most pervasive forms of fear operating in the world today. No matter what form negative and fear-based emotions express themselves, the final outcome is unhappiness, conflict and strife.

We will experience fear. It isn't "wrong" to have negative and fear-based emotions. At one time or another we experience many of these emotions. What is important is not to act on these emotions in such a way as to perpetuate them or let these feelings manifest in destructive and harmful actions over time. The challenge is to transcend them or transform them, to release them into the light, letting love, peace and forgiveness replace them. It isn't wrong to experience anger, but don't allow the anger to become a resentment, grudge or deep-seated hate. Acknowledge the feeling, seek to understand the fear beneath the feeling, and make a different choice.

As a runner, I daily run six miles. While running it isn't uncommon for increased adrenalin and endorphin production to stimulate long forgotten emotional memories to surface. Whether embarrassment, hurt, anger or emotional pain, these are re-experienced as though they just happened. It is truly amazing how vividly the emotional body retains the negative and fear-based emotions!

One time I relived an incident which occurred to me in the

fourth grade when I was humiliated by the teacher. I a same anger I felt such a long time ago. As I continue processed the fear beneath the hurt and anger, the false expectau. These included the idea the teacher shouldn't have embarrassed me, that she should have been fair, and that she shouldn't have singled me out when making a point of irritation she felt in general at the time. I allowed myself to consider other possibilities for her behavior, as well as the potential lessons for me.

I could then consciously and deliberately release the anger, hurt, pain and embarrassment into the light. I literally say "I release this anger, I release this hurt, I release all these negative and fear-based emotions into the light." I then say "I replace these negative and fear-based emotions with healing light, love, peace and forgiveness." As I do this, the negative feelings are gone, and positive feelings replace them.

It is natural to experience negative and fear-based emotions. It is inevitable in the course of a lifetime these feelings will occur. Especially during the formative years as we encounter parents, siblings, teachers and peers moments of hurt, embarrassment and pain are going to happen. The very process of learning how to live with others and become socialized to acceptable behavior brings anxious moments to our lives.

Learning to protect ourselves, young egos anticipate anxiety-producing situations. We learn to protect ourselves from vulnerable situations with fear. Sometimes we get trapped into facing all vulnerable or potentially risky situations by using protective behaviors or defenses as soon as we feel fear. Our minds become very good at anticipating fear.

However, as we grow and increase in awareness we have other options. As we make different choices we allow positive and love-based emotions to manifest for us more often. We can let positive and love-based emotions become the way we operate within ourselves, with others, and toward the world in general.

The foundation for giving and receiving love begins with self-love. As noted before, all healing begins with self-love and self-worth. When we decide to love ourselves we are saying we deserve to take care of ourselves. This isn't to be confused with being self-centered and narcissistic, for these are based on fear not love. Our society often mistakenly gives the message that self-love is egotistical.

True self-love is about nurturing and caring for ourselves, so we can meaningfully and intimately love and nurture others. We are only as capable of caring and sharing with others as we are of giving to ourselves.

Self-centeredness is fear-based, although still an attempt to find self-love. All fear-based emotions are a cry for love, distorted though they may be. When self-love is allowed and experienced, a sense of well-being and genuine peace comes over you, for then you feel centered, connected and well-grounded. With genuine self-love, we can accept feedback, evaluate it honestly, and make corrections in behavior and attitude, if needed, from a position of safety and security within ourself. A willingness to evaluate ourselves honestly, giving credit when credit is due, accepting praise as well as criticism, and allowing gentle self-criticism so we can do better naturally follow. We can indeed accept praise with proper humility.

As we experience self-love we are then able to more completely and easily express and share love with others. Love is meant to be given away. Love is meant to flow from us to all others and to all things. While it is easy to express love to the lovable, the far greater challenge is to share love with those we see as unlovable.

All major religions teach love at their core. Jesus said we are to love God with all our heart, mind and soul, and then love our neighbors as we love ourselves. We are to look beyond differences and surface behaviors, beholding the inner beauty and truth of another. Beneath the surface of each of us is the God-centered reality—the soul, Christ-consciousness, the God-In-Action-At-Each-Point. The salutation "namaste" elegantly states this truth, for it means the God in me salutes the God in you. Keep in mind all negative and fear-based emotions are a cry for love. We can then patiently see beyond the cry to the lovable within all.

Part of the larger challenge here is to move beyond conditional love to unconditional love. Too often we've learned to be conditional, putting demands onto others before we extend our love. As we learned to be protective of vulnerable feelings and hesitate to take risks with others, we place conditions on how, when, where and why we express and receive love.

Small children remind us of how to practice unconditional love, although they are fast learners when fear is connected to vulnerability. They openly express and share love at an early age, without regard to differences.

How often do we put conditions on giving and receiving love, even with those we feel most safe? Learning to give love freely, without conditions, is a very great challenge for all of us. It is a choice we can make at any time. As we strive to create and manifest joy, giving love unconditionally becomes an essential ingredient for achieving joy.

In spite of what many religions unfortunately or inadvertently teach, God is Pure Love, given unconditionally to all creation. Even the dark side receives unconditional and unceasing love. God knows even darkness will eventually return to the light. Behind darkness is always light.

Each time we feel connected to God, we experience the unending love He/She gives. During vision hypnosis, as clients connect with God and their divine spiritual heritage, the looks of pure joy and peace that passes all understanding radiate from their faces. I watch cleansing tears of joy stream down their faces as God's love touches them and transforms them. We all have that connection and can make conscious connection with God.

In meditation I have experienced the connection I have with God. It is a common experience in meditation, and another reason to make it a part of your life daily. Meditation does recharge our spiritual batteries.

Love can also be experienced with other dimensional beings in meditation. I have made connections with angels, my spirit guides, ascended masters, the Master Zeon, the Master Jesus, and Mother Mary. Always I experience unconditional love, streaming through them from God.

Part of adventurous living is to allow divine love to flow through us, unconditionally, wherever we are intuitively directed to express it. It's always a pleasure and joy when we are the recipient of such love, especially when it comes unexpectedly. When unexpected, a special feeling of warmth and belongingness results. When we experience love we create a connection between God and others through us, we become a true love connection.

God is Love, and the source of all love. This love is never fear-based or negative. God isn't judgmental or punitive. He has created a lawful universe to live in and in which we can experience the consequences of our choices. God is forever giving us love, even as we make free will choices which are the opposite of love. There is never condemnation and damnation, except as we create these for ourselves. We have an eternity to get it right.

As we allow love to flow through us we enhance our connection with God, and between God and all creation. We are meant to be companions with Him/Her. We become a conduit of love.

Love is felt. We know it emotionally. It flows in and through us, energizing and mobilizing us. It isn't enough to be the recipient of love, for it also has to be given. Love costs nothing to give, yet it's the most precious and valuable gift we can ever given. To hold love in and not express it outwardly is to deprive ourselves and others of this most magnificent gift. As we extend love, we extend healing and peace as well.

The healing effects of love occur in many ways. Countless stories are shared about the healing effects of love. Whether at the physical, mental, emotional or spiritual levels, the gift of love facilitates or creates healing. Well known is the gradual transformational healing which occurs with children when they are adopted and begin receiving love. Children in orphanages who are deprived of loving care don't thrive and achieve developmental milestones in a timely manner.

Elderly adults in nursing care facilities, when given love just by someone listening to them, begin to become lively and spontaneous again. Seeming senility in some adults, which is actually holding onto more joyful past memories, becomes current cognitive awareness and alertness when the gift of love is extended to them again.

Les Brown, motivational speaker and author, shares the story of his staff member, who is grotesquely disfigured by burns on 70% of his body, which resulted when he rescued a friend from an explosion and fire. He remains determined to extend and give his love to others and the world, as his mother has always given to him. After saving his friend, he was hospitalized for eight months, with little chance for survival initially. Many in similar circumstances die because no one is there to love them through their crisis.

Every day his mother came to be with him, nurturing him with her love, helping him to heal. With her as a role model, he gives his love unconditionally. Despite his disfigurement, and the unfortunate ridicule and no less painful stares of horror he continually encounters, he is a loving presence who gives of himself tirelessly. He said he made the decision to give love in honor of his mother, whose gift of love sustains him even in the darkest hours of his life.

I knew a man who lost half his face in combat during the Vietnam War. Reconstruction surgery did little to cover the horrendous disfigurement sustained in action. As a result he lost all his friends, and lost the opportunity for intimate, romantic love. Years later he experiences constant and ever increasing arthritic pain in his face.

He shared that when he was hit with the shell, he began to die and experienced an out-of-body experience. His description is similar to others' descriptions of the same phenomena with near death. He felt no pain and was completely at peace. He felt the serenity and freedom that comes as we move into spirit. Yet he was also aware of the unendurable pain his parents would feel about his death. In an instant he made the decision to return, sacrificing himself, ending up with constant pain and loneliness so that his parents would be spared his death. What an incredible gift of love went into his decision.

During vision hypnosis I have witnessed clients contacting deceased relatives. Love, forgiveness and resolution of past hurt and pain are often conveyed, bringing peace and healing to the client. On one occasion the deceased husband channeled through his wife, speaking directly to me, seeking reassurance his wife was going to be alright. He was reluctant to go to the light knowing how deeply she grieved for him. Once he was reassured, others in spirit came to direct him to the light. He left her his love and assurances of peace. She was relieved he was moving on, felt his love, but was also glad he was leaving as she intuitively sensed him hovering around her and was beginning to feel oppressed by his presence.

It costs nothing to give love. No longer hold back from experiencing and giving your love. Allow feelings of love to flow in and through you. Extend love to all of creation. Let God's love flow through you as well. Let peace and harmony triumph in your life and in the world. Adventurous living requires nothing less than freely sharing your love. Fill your life with love. Fill the world with love. Watch the joy that wells up in you.

CHAPTER TWELVE

FROM THE HEART

Adventurous living is the process of moving from a strictly intellectual orientation to a heart-centered orientation. It is the process of reconnecting the heart and the mind, allowing the heart to be the primary focus and direction in the process. This heart-mind orientation and approach allows us to function in full awareness, be intuitively connected, and make right decisions through the integration of the emotional and mental bodies.

The emotional body emphasis comes from the love which manifests in and through the heart center. When we first take something to our heart, and then from there to our mind, we will make the right choice that is for the highest good of all involved. We have more complete awareness and understanding at all levels, which facilitates decision making on the best course of action to take.

Furthermore, we are more connected to our Higher Self, and subsequently to God, allowing our true partnership with our Creator to be fully operational. Service to others and to creation comes from the heart, as love is brought into action in the right way. The heart-mind approach makes it more easy for the "still, small voice within" to be heard, direction can more easily be discerned, and partnership truly operates in our lives at all time. Joy naturally follows.

A physician colleague I work with is well known within the recovery community due to the service he provides others, always with dignity and compassion. He is a successful internist certified in addiction medicine. He treats addicted patients with genuine respect, not judging them harshly which too often occurs with treating professionals.

Not interested in people's mistakes, he works with them to find solutions to their addictions, and to the medical consequences of substance abuse. As a result of his patience, taking time to understand each client, as well as his diligence in finding solutions which will work, he is highly respected in the medical community as well as the recovery community. Due to his reputation, he receives many referrals from people in recovery.

His same attitude of patience, understanding, willingness to take time and work with people, and diligence in finding solutions extends to all the patients he works with and the medical difficulties they present. He is very scientifically oriented, with complete and thorough knowledge of medical science, biology, biochemistry and pharmacology.

Yet, what sets him apart as a healer is his attitude of service, the love and compassion he has for his patients, and the heart-mind connection he utilizes as he works his profession. Without realizing he does this, he approaches each patient from the heart. His care and concern motivate his analytic mind and intellectual ability to find the cause of a condition and to try the solutions which often successfully resolve the problem presented by the client. With substance abusers, this same approach from the heart first leads him to saying the right thing which often breaks through the minimization and denial dependence produces so healing may begin to occur.

One of his patients has experienced severe, chronic, debilitating headaches for the past three years. Many solutions and combinations of medicine have been tried, with only limited success. Not content to give up, working from his heart, he persists in analyzing and evaluating the person, instilling hope and confidence as he tries to find the solutions which will finally work. Even an early morning shower becomes a place he finds inspiration, thinking about this patient differently, entertaining new hypotheses and possible solutions.

The power of "from the heart" medicine can't be underestimated, for this patient knows he is important and worthy of the effort. This physician's attitude and effort continues to instill hope, even as depression, despair and hopelessness sometimes begin to overwhelm him.

The Western tradition emphasizes the intellect, and emphasizes the mind separate from our emotional and our intuitive natures. We are taught to focus on one-half our mind, the seat of reason and logic. We are taught to use only this part, even to the exclusion of our intuitive mind. Approaching life from only one part of the mind not only denies the intuitive part, but also the greater foundation of mind based on the positive, love-based emotions from the heart. We are meant to operate from the heart to the mind.

As we attempt to intellectually comprehend life on this planet, separate from the heart connection and our emotional and partnership link with God, we obviously misunderstand and fail to see the adventure life truly is. It is no wonder we struggle with the concept of faith, for faith is the knowingness which arises from the heart to a unified mind balanced between logic and intuition. Descartes stated "I think therefore I am." The truth is more like the following, "I come from my heart, therefore I AM." With my I AM connection through the heart center, or heart chakra, I AM fully able to reason and use my intuition.

It is interesting to note Descartes ended his famous line with the words "I am." For in each of us is the Mighty I AM Presence, our connection to God within. This I AM Presence is centered in our hearts. God, being Pure Love, naturally resides in the heart chakra. Our very soul, our eternal essence, our connection to our higher self is linked through the crown chakra to the heart chakra. The link comes down from our Higher Self, through the heart chakra of our physical self.

When we come from the heart we come from the divine within, the true spiritual nature which is the image and likeness of God in which we were created. Are we then surprised when reference is made to heart and soul? As we allow ourselves to enter in a heart-mind orientation and focus, we truly manifest the partnership with God that leads to successful and joyful living. This is what people in recovery learn about through the 12-step system of healing.

"From the heart" takes on new meaning as we remember we first came from love, the wisdom residing within which manifests through the subconscious mind. For we are then connected to Superconscious mind, as the heart-mind connection is completed. This connection is built on love. Christ consciousness emerges and operates as this process unfolds, opening us up to Universal Mind. The answer is love. Love is the key to the universe. From the heart we access love every time, and we get the answer we need every time we have a question or need direction.

Negative and fear-based emotions interface with love providing the answer from within so that all understanding can flow. Anger, resentment, vengeance and bitterness, all the negative emotions interfere with accessing the divine within each of us. They prevent true intellectual freedom from emerging.

Intellect, tempered by the love within, coming from the heart, provides true understanding and wisdom to be available to conscious awareness. This allows for choice which encompasses inner wisdom and intuitive perception.

Anger only creates enemies. It doesn't create solutions, facilitate awareness or promote growth individually or collectively. Anger sometimes has the limited capacity for survival to occur. Beyond that it only creates enemies and enmity.

When we come from the heart, when we allow love to be our guide, then right choices emerge. The outcome may not always appear to be the most desired for us at that moment in time. Others retain their free will to respond in their own way. The difference may only be for you and within you. Yet, from a different choice based on love, from the heart, the consciousness of all humanity shifts. Jesus' whole life was a demonstration of this principle, for he always operated from the heart, and a new understanding came to humanity and changed collective awareness.

We rarely live the truths he taught but they are there waiting for us to put them in action all the time. The consciousness of humanity elevated with Jesus' life. The same is true of all the other great teachers and masters who have assisted humanity, many of whom we know little or nothing about. In recent history, look at what Martin Luther King and Mahatmas Gandhi accomplished.

The heart-mind connection operates most effectively when there is an alignment of the heart chakra to the crown chakra. Chakras are the main energy centers of the body, with seven currently operating in the human body. As consciousness increases individually and collectively other energy centers will also come into operation.

The three lower chakras are the root or base chakra, located at the base of the spine; the navel chakra located in the lower abdomen; and, the solar plexus chakra located above the navel and below the chest. The rights associated with each of these chakras are the right to have, the right to feel and to pleasure, and the right to act.

When these three lower energy centers are brought into alignment, and energy from them is directed upward to the four higher chakras, then this energy is mobilized for the higher good and purpose of the individual.

The heart chakra, or fourth main energy vortex, is located in the center of the chest. Its function, according to the Legion of Light, is to anchor the life force from the Higher Self. In this connection "golden light" from the Higher Self enters the physical body through the crown chakra and flows through the heart chakra.

The qualities of the heart chakra are divine/unconditional love. The lessons are forgiveness, compassion, understanding, balance, group-consciousness, and oneness with life. Acceptance, peace, oneness, harmony and contentment come from the heart. Operating from the heart with these attributes qualifies intellect, tempering the errors of pure reason devoid of the universal wisdom which is accessed through the heart. The right to love and to be loved is associated with the heart chakra.

Continuing the alignment and flow of energy upward, the next energy vortex is the throat chakra. This chakra has to do with the power of the spoken word and true communication. It is the right to speak and to create. It has to do with integration, peace, truth, knowledge, wisdom, loyalty, honestly, reliability, gentleness and kindness.

The next highest chakra is the brow chakra, also known as the third eye energy center. It is the right to see. It's qualities are soul realization, intuition, insight and imagination. It has to do with clairvoyance, concentration, peace of mind, wisdom, devotion, and perception beyond duality.

Completing the heart-mind connection through the alignment and flow of energy through the upper centers is the crown chakra. This is located at the top of the head. It is the right to know. It is the unification of the Higher Self with the human personality. It has to do with oneness with the infinite. Its qualities include spiritual will, inspiration, unity, divine wisdom and understanding. Its lessons include idealism, selfless service, perception beyond space and time, and continuity of consciousness.

The heart-mind connection unifies these four centers, allowing the Higher Self from above and within, anchored to the heart, to manifest the qualities of unconditional love, true communication, soul realization, and unification of the Higher Self with the human personality. Coming from the heart allows God to speak in and through us.

As we come from the heart we allow ourselves to know and to express the unity which exists, to know we are truly one, making right choices and taking right action. It is the guidance of the Higher Self which always has complete understanding of the divine plan through the "Mighty I AM Presence" in each of us.

When we speak from the heart others can't mistake the sincerity, the humility or the wisdom that pours forth. Motivational speakers such as Og Mandino or the late Norman Vincent Peale continually demonstrate this.

Og Mandino always speaks from the heart. Simple, yet eloquent, he conveys warmth, caring, sensitivity, depth and extreme joy. A special time of the year at the Church of Today is when he visits to share his annual Christmas story. He likes to tell us to close our eyes and listen, for "Grandpa Og has another story for you." His stories always capture the essence of Christmas, as well as the underlying truths of life.

One year's story told of a child and his 95 year old neighbor. She lived so long she survived all her family and friends, and was pretty much alone. The neighbor boy would take over to the neighbor's house the groceries his mother would buy her each week. In the house he would help her arrange the shelves as she put the groceries away. She would always pay him even though he tried not to take the money.

Since it was the Christmas season the boy was determined not to take the money this time, as his gift to her was the service he would provide. The week of Christmas it had just snowed and he was eager and excited to play in the snow. Yet he took time to help her with the groceries once again, and although he really wanted to be outside, he patiently listened as she told stories of her youth. She especially loved to tell him about the snow covered church she went to as a child, out in the middle of the woods near her home.

Before he left that day the woman pressed a quarter in his hand, even though he tried to leave without her paying him. When he arrived at the store, eager to spend his extra treasure, worth a lot in his day, he happened upon a Christmas card with a snow covered church in the woods pictured upon it. Without hesitation he bought the card, filled it out, and took it back to the woman as his gift to her.

Several weeks later the old woman died. Found on the night stand next to her bed, amongst very few mementos, was the card he gave her. He had touched her with his love, and gave her the greatest gift of all. The child came from his heart and gave in ways he didn't comprehend until much later in his life.

Told with deep emotion, Og Mandino himself gave us the gift of love that day as he shared the story from his own heart. If all the world would begin to think and act from the heart, this planet could literally be transformed over night. We could become a place of peace, understanding, love and beauty in the "twinkling of an eye."

One of the most beautiful and loving demonstrations of the principle of from the heart came from the classmates of my nephew after his father died. My younger brother suddenly died the day after celebrating his 43rd birthday. His son's schoolmates made cards of sympathy and condolence for his loss. The cards are marvelous in their simplicity of love and support, yet contain the wisdom of the ages in spite of the ages of the children, 2nd graders at the time.

Some of the children shared their understanding of death from their own recent experiences with their own families' acquaintances. One girl also experienced the death of a family member recently. Another girl told my nephew she "knew" what he was going through because her uncle, grandfather, younger sister and a cousin's baby all just died recently. With all those losses she was the most supportive and understanding in her expression of love and concern, speaking deeply from her heart even at such a young age.

Many children drew pictures of my brother in heaven, or rising up to be in heaven. From their hearts, these children have a rudimentary grasp of eternal life and of the ascension process. One child even drew a picture of my brother on one page, then on the next page, showed the bottom of his feet at the top of the page, demonstrating the ascension process as we move into a higher vibrational body. Such wisdom in young children!

One girl with partial Native American heritage shared how her grandfather's spirit returned to be with the Great Spirit, and assured my nephew my brother did the same. Whether in drawings or writing, these children have a tremendous capacity of understanding what death is really all about.

While they knew and acknowledged the sorrow and pain my nephew and his family were going through, they also conveyed from the heart the wisdom and truth that life is eternal, that the spirit of the person continues on, and that eventually ascension is accomplished by all. They also "knew" other spirits would be there to greet my brother, and they "knew" some day his son will be reunited with his father. Their love and concern, expressed so deeply and lovingly from their hearts, was truly touching and therapeutic for all of us. To this day when I look at these cards I experience joy, wonderment and gratitude for their heart-felt sharing.

Children have a wonderful capacity to approach the world in wonderment and joy. Often they operate from the heart as they seek to know and understand the world about them. Developmentally they can also be quite self-centered and impulsive, and certainly need our loving guidance to learn how to live with others in a cooperative and harmonious manner. The challenge of all parenting is to provide firm limits and guidance without stifling this wonder and joy, this sense of adventure and purpose all children possess. Discipline and limit-setting is only ten percent of parenting, the rest is loving nurturance and teaching.

Each of us continues to possess an inner child that recalls and knows the wonderment, joy and adventurous spirit we come into this world with. Our inner child continues to possess the simplicity of wisdom and understanding from the heart. With guidance and loving support we easily keep our inner child readily available.

Otherwise, we must some how become reacquainted with this part of ourselves. Many paths are suggested from books, the worlds of literature and the arts, films, numerous paths of wisdom and truth, therapies, and meditations and other processes which facilitate inner understanding, awareness and re-awakening.

When we come from the heart we allow Divine Love and the wisdom of our Higher Self to guide and direct us. An adventurous attitude and approach readily emerges as we let unconditional love, compassion, kindness and calm gentleness guide our thoughts and actions. We live in and respond to the world about us with greater awareness and understanding, moving away from disharmony and conflict toward harmony and peace.

We react differently to the world, for we know the outer appearances don't define the truth of a person or situation. Even when danger is present we are safely guided around the danger.

When we come from the heart we trust intuition, and listen to the still, small voice within. We let our Higher Self guide us and direct us to right action and right choice.

When we come from the heart we let others know we acknowledge and understand their experience. We are able to successfully convey this understanding. We know who they are and who we are.

Adventurous living is based on understanding many basic truths. It is about attitude, a joyful and adventurous attitude, as we approach and deal with life. Learning to come from the heart, to put reason and logic in their proper perspective, tempered by the wisdom of Divine Love working through our hearts, we truly do understand and know how to approach life. Inner wisdom can then strengthen and guide us.

The heart-mind connection brings compassion to reason, allowing the human personality to exist in its proper place, so the spiritual being we are can operate at all levels of existence. With joy, positive and love-based emotions become the driving forces in our lives.

CHAPTER THIRTEEN

SERVICE

As we understand and apply basic truths we begin to let our light shine within. Guy Lynch, previous Senior Minister at the Church of Today, states the following, "Let the light shine within you, for as you do your light shines for all of humanity." As our light shines we light the way for humanity and for the world. As we live our truth the light within magnifies and guides us in service to all.

As we become increasingly aware and begin to "know," understanding basic truths, we advance in our ability to apply basic truth. As we begin to receive, feel and give love, the next step in adventurous living readily emerges—being of service. The Unity Hymn shared in an earlier chapter begins with the greatest thing in all of life is knowing God, then moving to loving God, and finally serving God. This succinctly summarizes how we move from understanding to application and finally to service.

The attitude of service and the activity of service put into action our part of the Divine Plan, in every area of our lives. Being of service enables us to be of benefit to all we touch and to the world as a whole. Service is the expression of love from us to all of creation. Service is truly allowing God's Love to work in and through us.

From the very smallest acts to the grandest expression of giving to others, service is an attitude which allows us to extend ourselves to others and assist them in lightening the load they carry in life. Service is an attitude that simply asks the questions of how I may be of assistance to others. With the questions of how I may be of service constantly before us, we are able to be divinely guided in saying and doing those things that help another in their struggle, make their day brighter, help them to learn and grow, and ultimately demonstrate to others the positive possibilities that exist for everyone.

Father Leo Booth has given us a modern version of the 23rd Psalm which goes like this:

God is my friend. What more could I want?
God sits with me in the quiet times in my life.
God calls me forth as a whole person.
Even though I walk along paths of pain,
prejudice, hatred and depression,
my fears are quieted because God is with me.
God's words and thoughts challenge me.
God causes me to be sensitive to the needs of
mankind, then lifts up opportunities for serving.
God's confidence stretches me.
Surely love will be mine to share
throughout my life, and I shall be sustained
by God's concern forever.

While more than just service is mentioned here, it is an integral part of the whole process. Allowing ourselves to be more sensitive to the needs of others, opportunities to serve naturally arise and present themselves.

Of the many definitions provided for the word service, the one meant here is acts of assistance or benefit. Within the larger context of universal truths another definition also applies here, acts of devotion to God. For in providing acts of assistance or benefit, with an attitude of giving of ourselves and extending ourselves, true devotion to God is made manifest. It is not enough to profess beliefs in universal truth, for we are not known only by what we say but also by what we do. Actions do speak louder than words. We are to put our beliefs into action. Service is belief in action.

Adopting an attitude of service in all activities is putting belief into action in all spheres of our life. From the very simple daily acts of smiling at others, opening a door, or offering to help in some small way to the greatest acts one can conceive and employ, an attitude of service gives assistance, eases another's burden, and brings peace and joy to that corner of the world.

Service is not restricted to great acts of courage, volunteerism or altruism. Service is an on-going, all-encompassing, way-of-being expressed in all levels in all activities. It is thoughtfulness and purpose, using time wisely and patiently to bring all of ourselves to others and the world about us.

Service begins with the everyday activities we engage in. It begins with family as we assist the loved ones we live with. Completing activities of daily living without reminder or prompting is a good beginning. From there, it is becoming aware of what needs to be done around the house, and going ahead and doing it. It expands to include offers of assistance to others without expectation of reciprocation.

Service is calling parents, siblings and family members regularly, and taking genuine interest in their activities and interests. It is actively listening, and being patient when we want to rush ahead to do what we want. It is about compromise and sharing, letting others lead when we always want to lead, and letting ourselves lead when all we want to do is follow. Service with family is offering to help, yet letting others do what they must to also learn and grow.

Service expands next to encompass friends and neighbors. Helping out when needed, being available to listen and share, and offering guidance and support all flow from an attitude of service. I remember a neighbor from our Lincoln Park days who was first an acquaintance and then a friend. He was an alcoholic, was sometimes critical of others, and engaged in interests I did not always share. Yet it was okay to talk and share with him, and to patiently listen when his opinions or views were opposite of mine.

Service was being there for him as a neighbor, offering patience and the willingness to listen. At times service was returned as well, whether lending a tool, clearing snow from our sidewalk, or taking in our mail when we were away. I was honored to be of service when he died, serving as a pallbearer at his funeral. I am always honored when asked to do this, for anyone. Once he was gone, our friendship with his wife grew even greater. Our family enjoyed clearing her snow in the winter, helping her with heavy yard work if needed, or sending over extra waffles on a weekend morning.

The neighbors on the other side also gave with an attitude of service with us from time to time. A retired couple, they always gave a friendly wave, even through windows. We engaged in long summer conversations as they sat on their back porch. As my son grew, the man always took interest in him and talked to him each day. He enjoyed sharing his wisdom and friendly love with him. Neither neighbors ever forgot to greet and pet our dogs, bringing service even to our pets. When my son was born, and later at times when my wife was sick, the one neighbor, Italian in heritage, always sent over plates of pasta to ease our way. What a wonderful treat it was enjoying homemade Italian food at that time.

With the birth of our son, we got to know and become friends with neighbors behind us. Gradually we came to be included in their family, even celebrating the Spanish custom of Migas with them every year at Christmas. Service meant we helped each other move when the time came to move on. Service also meant we were there to help a depressed and lonely daughter trying to face her problems and move into a more positive way of being in the world.

Service then expands to involve colleagues and coworkers wherever we work. Being supportive and helpful, pitching in even when we don't have to, and avoiding gossip and politics is all part of service with colleagues and coworkers. Friendliness, support, and interest in the parts of their lives they are willing to share is essential. Being there for them in their times of crisis and suffering is service.

Attending their funerals, visiting them and their loved ones in hospitals and contributing to office funds meant to help or send them on with thanks come from an attitude of service. Sharing ideas, listening without criticizing, or a simple smile bring service to the work place. Actively helping and contributing in causes supported by coworkers comes from service.

Expanding further, service to companies, clients and customers, internal and external, brings harmony, productivity and success to all. This benefits you as well as all others. Service is giving 100%, doing your very best and helping the larger vision and mission of your work place emerge. All of us delight in stores and salesclerks that work with an attitude of service.

In negotiating a contract, an attitude of service works toward a solution that is best for all involved. In sports, it is an attitude of doing one's very best for the good of the team, while at the same time never at the expense of an opponent. Contrast this with too many of today's athletes who revel in their own play at the expense of all others. How many athletes forget an attitude of service extends to the fans, when it is so easy to sign an autograph or act friendly. Giving our very best in an attitude of service leads to success in all career endeavors.

Volunteer work becomes the ultimate expression of service, as we give our time and effort to assist our religious organization, a charity, or one in need. Helping to make an organization to function efficiently and effectively, as well as serve those who benefit from their activity is part of service. But service is also volunteering to help in less structured and organized situations as well.

I have watched a neighbor flourish and grow after the death of her husband by volunteering at the local hospital. I have watched a colleague and friend grow as she volunteered at our church, now in service as a head usher. I observed with quiet pride as my father volunteered to assist at the same church, giving guest speakers rides to and from the airport, running money from church collections to the bank, helping a cancer-ridden lady get a ride to the Thanksgiving day service and dinner, or visiting a dying member in the hospital, giving them aid and comfort as they left this planet.

Service is an expression of love. We are directed by God to be of service. All the master teachers have emphasized service to others. Jesus demonstrated this truth by washing the feet of his disciples and friends, which was considered a great act of humility in his day.

Humility is an essential ingredient in the act of service. Compassion is also an essential ingredient in the act of service. For to best serve and assist is with deep compassion in our hearts, mind and soul. It is a depth of love that guides each of us to be of true service in this world.

With the death of my father, the greatest gift I received during the initial sad time was the stories of service I learned about by my father, as well as the service offered by friends and acquaintances of my father and of me. Unfortunately, deaths in families often bring out the worst in people, and regrettably the same happened in our family. Fortunately, deaths also bring out the very best in people and family members, and the same happened in my family as well.

The attitude of service which came from my wife was of great assistance during the first few days. A source of comfort and strength, she quietly went along adding the little touches that eased all of our pain. Constantly attentive and listening, she was available to me if I needed her strength and love. I simply knew it was quietly there for me. She arranged the bagels, cookies, mints and beverages to be available to all family members, and shared with friends at the funeral home.

My father- and mother-in-law came from Pittsburgh, and with the attitude and action of service, were of great assistance to us in our time of need. They were at our sides throughout the funeral, helping us at home and at the viewing. They spent time providing comfort, but went way beyond this as well. At the viewing they spoke to and listened to the many people who came, even the family and friends of my brothers who had difficulty being present most of the time themselves.

The attitude of service displayed by friends, colleagues and coworkers was deeply touching to me personally. The number of people who made time in their busy schedules to visit me and/or to attend the memorial service left me in awe and with great gratitude. That so many of my friends, acquaintances, colleagues and coworkers offered me comfort in my time of need truly expressed the principal of service to others. It made a difficult time more tolerable, and gave to me so much love which will always be with me.

Beyond this, the people who took time to send cards and to write notes demonstrated the wonders of service in action. I never truly appreciated how taking time to buy a card, write a note, and send it could make so much difference in a life at a moment in time. A little effort and time can be the most important thing one can do to ease the pain of another. Service can be as grand as a simple act of kindness.

Service was also former neighbors and friends of my father taking time to be of comfort, pay their respects, and honor my father. By honoring him they were of service to the family, helping us to ease our initial pain and deal with the shock of suddenly losing one we so deeply loved. Taking time out of their busy lives to help us in our time of need is service in action.

One special moment of service came from a friend from high school and college. In the years since college I have seen him once at our 25th high school reunion. Ironically, I accidentally ran into him at the Michigan-Wisconsin football game. He came over to greet my father who was with me that day. Having learned about my Dad's death from his wife, who saw the obituary, he came to the viewing at the funeral home.

After a long, busy day with his law practice, and then a squash game with a friend, he took time to come to the funeral home before going home to his wife and children. It was out of the way, but an attitude of service allowed him to make the time to comfort an old friend when he could have easily just gone home.

One of the positive outcomes of my father's death was the opportunity to learn how he was of service to people individually. Many of the people who came to the funeral home or to the memorial service recounted the ways Dad was of service to others. Whether simply a passing thought that stayed with the person, or a more connected relationship, service was manifested by Dad in many ways. Many people enjoyed sharing my father's trademark comment, "Have a nice day, choose it." With a simple statement he reminded others of universal truth, our attitude creates the kind of day we will have.

Several people knew Dad from a Course in Miracles study group. Many appreciated his commitment to that group. Offering his own insights and the awareness of the Course, he illuminated its truth for others.

Beyond this, one young man shared how Dad was like a father to him. Lacking a father-figure in his life, he had come to view Carl as a surrogate father. Apparently Dad took this young man under his care emotionally and psychologically, providing nurturance, support and guidance. Genuine loss was expressed by this young man as he shared how Dad assisted him, and made a difference in his life.

Others spoke about the love, care and guidance they received from Dad. They spoke about how they again found meaning and purpose in their lives, often when they were near losing hope or when life seemed to be beating them down. Many peoples' lives were touched by Dad as they came to know him at the various support groups he was involved with.

Approaching each person nonjudgmentally and with an attitude of service, Dad allowed himself to be the catalyst that led to self-love, self-worth and ultimately self-healing. He did not shy away from startling people with gentle but blunt statements of truth, but with an attitude of service I suspect these were mostly well received.

The number of people who came to honor Dad and to share with his family the impact he made on their lives was truly amazing given the short notice of his death and the scheduling of the viewing and memorial service. Equally amazing was the network of informal contact which went into action getting the word to many diverse people, even to a support group for recently widowed, divorced or separated adults he was involved with a few years earlier. Service was demonstrated by all these people who took the time to call around and let as many of his friends and acquaintances as possible know about his death and the memorial service.

Ironically, Dad's last activity was to spend time at the Church of Today's volunteer pot luck Christmas party. He was with the people he loved and enjoyed, at a place that was a second home for him, as well as a source of inspirational and support for himself. People who spent the last hours with him reported he was outgoing and sharing, with no hint his time of transition was so near. He spent his last moments being of service, continuing to share truth with others in his customary blunt, but gentle style.

In honor of Dad, the singles group at the Church of Today collected money that was donated to an adopted family that Christmas. Service as simple as donating a few dollars a piece so that a needy family could have a nicer Christmas is a real tribute to the service Dad provided.

Finally, in the interest of being of better service to others, Dad learned how to do hypnosis in the last two years of his life. He became certified in hypnosis so he could assist others in overcoming harmful habits, enhance performance in certain areas of their lives which interfered with maximum growth and awareness currently. He was avidly interested in and supportive of my own hypnotherapy work and discoveries, especially vision hypnosis.

Service—both as an attitude and as an action—makes a difference in our lives. Not only does service enhance our own growth, development and awareness, but it also makes a difference in the lives of people we come in contact with. Whether random acts of kindness with perfect strangers, or more intense, involved activity with one individual or group, service makes a difference.

With an orientation to service we can and do make a difference with others and with this planet. The healing and transformation of this planet comes from individual service, both in thought and action. As we give service, our corner of the world becomes healed, and the collective consciousness of humanity moves forward. Peace, harmony and love are possible. The transformation begins with you, as you move from being a taker to being a giver. Be of service. Heal yourself, heal others, heal the world. You DO make a difference.

CHAPTER FOURTEEN

THE PATH OF JOY

Life is meant to be joyful. It is also meant to be extraordinary. We aren't meant to live ordinary lives, or worse yet, lives of quiet desperation. Life is ultimately a great spiritual adventure, as we seek to know truth and to apply it in our lives. As we meet individual and collective challenges true joy emerges. We heal and grow physically, mentally, emotionally and spiritually. We learn to operate from our heart so we can fulfill our part in the Divine Plan. Ultimately we learn how to live in physicality, operating from our spiritual heritage so we can be co-creators with God.

We live in a wonderful universe. In spite of all its challenges, adversities, painful realities, suffering and temptations, we also live on a wonderful planet. It is a planet on which we can manifest true joy and happiness. As we live the adventure of meeting challenges, adversities, painful realities, sufferings and temptations, we experience self-healing, growth, development and awareness.

As we live the adventure of positive experiences, opportunities and pleasant realities, joy also emerges. The adventure of life is about discovery—to become more aware, to find and live truth principles, and to manifest our spiritual heritage in human form.

As we understand and apply basic truths we enter the path of joy. We learn how to make our heart sing. Cynthia Hacinli shares the story of a New England antiques dealer who exemplifies the joyful life. In an article, entitled "Stuff To Make The Heart Sing," she shares how Polly Blake follows her intuition to select unusual antiques others overlook. Polly is quoted as saying, "Oh, it's a great adventure."

Along with her husband "Bear" she looks for what makes her smile. As a result, they have developed something of a reputation with decorators seeking that offbeat accent. She sums up her approach to her business, which is also her approach to life. She says she looks for the unusual things that make her heart sing. The keys to adventurous living are contained in the attitudes of people like Polly.

Everything in life is an adventure. The keys to adventurous living are contained in many places. They are contained in the pages of this book. They are contained in understanding basic truths to create joy. They come in understanding there are no coincidences, that life is serendipitous. This includes painful realities, and how these painful realities can serve our greater good.

They come in recognizing life's lessons for us, both generally and specifically. Becoming aware of life's lessons and how they apply to each of us provides further keys. They come in understanding universal laws and how these laws operate. Discovering our mission, and how this mission serves the divine plan provides more keys to adventurous living. Certainly understanding God's plan for us provides keys to ways in which adventurous living can manifest in our lives.

Adventurous living comes in our relationships with others, especially those who are enemies or foes. Learning how to heal conflict with others, accepting the opportunity for learning they provide, and implementing laws of forgiveness and grace provide one key to adventurous living.

Keys to adventurous living are contained in understanding how we think creates the world we live in. The importance of master mind principles in creating the world we live in is fundamental to the adventurous attitude. Having gratitude for all the opportunities, blessings and challenges continue to provide keys. Manifesting love, providing service, and being centered in the God-connection within the heart provides guidance that allows adventurous living to come forth.

As we apply the keys of adventurous living, we meet challenges, become increasingly more aware, provide self-healing at all levels and discover and live truth principles. An attitude of expectation and of joy begins to emerge. We remember our true heritage and begin to understand why we chose to come and live in the illusion of three-dimensional physicality.

Life is meant to be joyful. However, as we enter the illusion of the three-dimensional life, and gradually forget our true heritage and connection with all realms, we begin to believe only what we perceive with our physical senses. We also begin to believe only what our reason and ego tell us is the reality in this world. We become fearful and allow negativity to manifest. We begin to believe happiness comes from outside ourselves, through money, possessions, status, power and the right lover.

The process of rediscovery puts us on the path of joy. Numerous steps on the path of joy bring us back to full awareness, atunement, and at-one-ment. As we progress along these steps we experience increasing joy. The very process, not the destination, brings joy into our lives.

The first step on the path of joy is self-healing. Each one of us requires healing from the illusion we have believed in, which subsequently left us with spiritual, mental, emotional and physical scars. Those scars are not permanent fixtures on our psyche. They can be transformed by the healing process. As they transform, awareness and growth do occur. The transformational process takes us beyond limitation to full possibility.

As stated several times in this book, all healing begins with self-love and self-worth. The process begins with developing self-esteem. We are given many messages from parents, siblings, family members, peers, teachers and authority figures it is self-centered and narcissistic to love ourselves. We are taught we have to be concerned about others first, and sacrifice ourselves for others.

The truth is genuine self-love and self-worth leads to more loving, caring and genuine relationships with others. It also leads to "tough love," which is the capacity to say "no" to others attempts to manipulate and control us. If you find yourself being pressured to do something you don't want to do, or to feel something different than what you feel, then manipulation is occurring. Why should what someone else wants be more important than what you need or want for yourself? With positive self-esteem, you learn to choose based on your own "Inner Supreme Court."

Nathaniel Brandon has studied self-esteem and written many books about what self-esteem is and how to develop it. You are invited to learn more about this by reading his books. For purposes of this book I have summarized his key points, what he calls the six pillars of self-esteem.

He states the essence of self-esteem is to trust our mind and to know we are worthy of happiness. Since mind is connected to God, self-esteem is the essence of our God connection. Achieving high self-esteem is something we can accomplish.

When our self-respect is contingent on what others think and feel, we get into trouble. Fear enters in, especially the fear of what others think. Then we end up believing we are diminished or somehow less. As we get in touch with who we really are, and devote our attention to our issues, then self-esteem occurs. Trying to fix others or please others will not get us there.

Nathaniel Brandon states what is important in our existence is the judgment we pass on ourselves. This affects the kind of life we will create for ourselves. Our competence and worth define the kind of goals we have, how we will do our job, the quality of our relationships, and how we relate to our families—what we will become. The way we feel inwardly, how we deeply feel and think about ourselves shapes the life we create for ourselves.

According to Brandon, self-esteem is two things. First, it is the confidence we have in our ability to cope with the basic challenges of life. Second, it is the confidence in our right to be happy, or confidence in our right to be worthy of happiness. Self-esteem is an achievement, something we can build, learn and create. It is the opposite of inadequacy, self-doubt and not feeling worthy enough.

High self-esteem is the first thing we can do for ourselves. Self-love and self-worth, the basis of all healing, develops as we employ six principles of action. These principles, outlined by Brandon, are the most important for self-esteem. They are:

1. The practice of living consciously.
2. The practice of self-acceptance.
3. The practice of self-responsibility.
4. The practice of self-assertiveness.
5. The practice of living purposefully.
6. The practice of personal integrity.

Living consciously is using our mind and it's ability to think.

It is valuing this ability to think over unconsciousness. It is a great passion to learn. It is about making sense out of life and experiences. It is an awareness of mistakes, and correcting them immediately. It is being present in our relations, and being present in the moment. It is about being in reality—that is, responsible to our reality.

Self-acceptance, the second principle, is learning not to be in adversarial relationships to ourselves. It is accepting all of our thoughts, feelings and action, including negative and fear- based ones. It is about complete honesty about ourselves. It is avoiding denial, self-deception, self-disowning and self-repudiation.

When we reject ourselves or part of ourselves, and when we don't accept ourselves, we can't change the parts that are negative and fear-based. We deprive ourselves of the opportunity for genuine self-forgiveness. Self-acceptance is the precondition of change, because we can honestly forgive ourselves our faults and correct them.

The third principle for developing positive self-esteem is taking responsibility for our life and our well-being. It is "I" who chooses, decides and takes action. We are responsible for the level of consciousness we bring to our relationships. Self-responsibility is the conscientiousness we bring to our work, for the words which come out of our mouths, and for our personal happiness. No one is going to make life right for us, nor are they going to heal our past. Self-responsibility is knowing we have to do something different to get better, to become mature and express wisdom, to live truth principles.

Assertiveness is the ability to practice self-expression. It is the willingness to put ourselves into life, into reality around us, to express our thoughts and feelings. It is the capacity to be authentic and genuine. It is respecting our own thoughts and feelings, to live them in the world, and not to hide them out of fear or disapproval. It is the courage to be, rather than lying, disowning ourselves, or concealing ourselves because somebody won't agree or approve. Self-assertiveness is being who we are with honesty, integrity and dignity. It isn't an excuse for being rude and mistreating others, for assertiveness can be done gently and firmly.

Living purposefully is establishing goals so we live and fulfill our mission. It is manifesting our partnership with God so the Divine

Plan unfolds through our goals and purposes. This is a four step process. The first step is to formulate goals in every area of our lives. Step two is to develop a plan on how we are going to achieve these goals. The third step is to monitor all of our actions to see if they are in alignment with our goals and plans. The final step is to pay attention to outcomes, to make sure what we are doing will work to achieve our goals. In this way we turn wants into conscious purposes, allowing for the power of positive self-esteem to emerge. We manifest joy through a life that works.

The final principle that Brandon outlines is the practice of personal integrity. Integrity is being wise, rational and choosing the moral thing to do. It is avoiding hypocrisy. It is being integrated in thoughts, values, professed convictions and behavior. It is walking the talk, keeping the promises, telling the truth, keeping commitments, pursuing values one admires, and avoiding things not admired. It is congruence between what one does and what one says.

What feels good is not necessary for self-esteem to emerge. Outward things such as money, the car we drive, popularity, conquests or power may feel good, but will not lead to self-esteem. To be happy is to be serene inwardly. We are responsible for our own self-esteem. This responsibility can be our burden, but it can also be our glory.

We are extraordinary beings. As we manifest self-love and self-worth we allow the true capacity and truth of ourselves to emerge. We begin the process of healing and ultimately of transformation. We allow the truth of our being, the "inner child within" to re-emerge. Although this inner child may be wounded by adversity, challenge and trauma it is readily healed. Self-love and self-worth allow this healing to take place, and allow our spiritual being to completely have and enjoy the human experience.

Healing first begins at the spiritual level as we rediscover our heritage and let this heritage guide us. We let our spiritual nature emerge and gently guide us through all the adventures life has to offer. We reconnect with God and allow the part of God within us to direct our lives.

The twelve step tradition for healing addictions begins with this very premise, when we surrender to our Higher Power and recognize of ourselves we can do nothing. Being spiritual isn't to be confused with being religious, although they can and often do overlap. Spiritual healing is reconnecting with the God Presence within us.

Spiritual healing is allowing the "Mighty I AM Presence" in us to fully operate in our lives. Calling on this "Magic Presence" leads to perfect choices and actions. It is continual right guidance.

The I AM commands we decree, consciously or unconsciously, create the results we have in our lives. If the commands are negative, such as I Am no good, or I Am not capable of happiness, this is what will arise. Commands that I Am successful, prosperous, joyful, and in oneness with all that is will create these results. For further understanding of the I AM process, you are directed to the St. Germain literature and to I AM temples and groups.

Mental healing occurs as we recognize that right thought and belief creates the world we live in. Learning to use our mental capacity in full service to our greater good, and not to the limiting beliefs of the ego, is important here. As consciousness expands, we are then able to use greater portions of the mind's capacity, especially higher levels where what has been termed paranormal activity resides.

During the historical period humankind lost the abilities of greater mind. Deja vu experiences, which many people experience, are only a glimpse of the greater abilities higher mind is capable of. Psychic ability, lucid dreaming, prophetic dreaming and visions, clairvoyance, clairaudience, and much more are the tools available to us and meant for our use when we heal and develop mentally. Ultimately, supermind ability awaits us.

Healing at the emotional level begins as previous hurts, pains, emotional scars and traumas are resolved. As they are resolved greater understanding and awareness of the greater good they served arises as we recognize how they facilitated our growth and development.

As negative and fear-based emotions are released, and replaced with positive and love-based emotions, previous painful and difficult events are transformed. Ultimately, as we forgive others and ourselves, true healing of the emotional self and the emotional body is accomplished. Forgiving ourselves and others is so important Jesus devoted a considerable part of his ministry teaching these concepts. As we learn why and how to forgive, we can truly operate from the heart, allowing God's universal love to work in and through us.

Finally, physical healing can be accomplished as self-love and self-worth are focused on physical conditions. As Louise Hay and others have shown us, there is meaning to each and every illness and disorder, and mental and emotional components to every disease. Illness is dis-ease, a reflection of disharmony and discord within.

Injury and illness may also be placed within our genetic code with our permission prior to our birth in physical form, so the soul can learn how to heal our physical self, or to provide the obstacle, hurdle or experience which will facilitate our growth at all levels.

One winter I developed a foot injury which interfered with my daily running and one way I maintain weight control. Without this form of exercise I began to gain weight. A friend who provides accupressure healing was consulted. During the session she described my foot "talking" to her. The messages were the injury was meant to occur at the time it did so I would begin weight control based on proper nutrition and diet, not just relying on exercise to control weight. In addition my body also told her it was time to move further toward a vegetarian diet. This injury became an opportunity to manifest self-healing at the physical level.

The first step on the path of joy is multitudinous, as we work on healing at all levels. Yet the process of healing and developing self-love and self-worth in an of itself provides joyful experiences.

The next step on the path of joy is to live life impeccably. This means being true to ourselves and the values we live by. Shakespeare said, "To thine own self be true." Impeccable living is the practice of personal integrity, full awareness, and complete atunement to universal truth and divine guidance.

As we live impeccably there will be inevitable shortcomings and failures. We are not perfect nor are we meant to be perfect. We each have our own foibles and inconsistencies. Certainly our enemies like to point these out, trying to negate our truth, confusing our mistakes with the core truth of our being. Impeccable living is living more and more in a perfected state of being. However, we are all in various stages of getting there. When we arrive there, we no longer need to live on this or similar three-dimensional planets.

Impeccable living is about creating peace and harmony. It is about having a reverence for all life. It is about oneness so all live in peace and freedom in a world we manifest together. It is about reaching into a place of peace and love for all. It is about being a spiritual warrior, living in our truth and in universal truth.

It is about taking out of ourselves criticism, blame, resistance, judging, rebellion, jealousy, self-pity, pride, selfishness, doubt and fear. It is about living the Ten Commandments.

The next step on the path of joy is to live adventurously facing the challenges which come our way. It is about dealing with all life's challenges. It is about deciding and choosing, taking risks, and the willingness to fail. It is about being proactive, rather than passive or reactive, never choosing, or letting others and events have power over you. It is about empowering yourself, not victimization.

The final step on the path of joy is making the most of each and every moment. It is about being in the moment, fully appreciating all we have and are, accepting each part of the adventure, even the problems, adversities and painful realities. Problems move us forward. Jack Boland was often fond of saying, "If you don't have a problem right now, go out and find one."

Making the most of each moment is finding joy in what is all around us. It is taking time to be aware of and appreciate what is available to us. It is the joy of Spring unfolding, a soft and gentle winter snow, the beauty of birds singing their wondrous songs, the delighted laughter of small children at play, the lined wisdom of an elderly person's face, all the beauty which is around us when we take the time to see what is "really" there.

It is enjoying the tranquility and healing energy of the forest, the sound of a brook as the water playfully glides by, the delightful sound of leaves blowing in the wind, the sound and fury of a summer storm. It is the sweet aroma of bread baking, the cool delicious taste of ice cream on a hot summer day. It is anything and everything. It is all the things we learn to enjoy, and the adventure of seeing everything as a source of joy. For joy is inside us, as we become fully and completely alive.

As we follow these steps and live adventurously joy emerges. As we understand and apply basic truths, form our partnership with God, think and act from the heart, and live from love we begin to experience joy attacks. We begin to feel so good we can hardly stand it.

As joy enters our lives we begin to experience symptoms of inner peace, what Jesus called the peace that passes all understanding. Saskin Davis identifies some of the symptoms of inner peace as these:

-A tendency to think and act spontaneously rather than on fears based on past experiences.
-An unmistakable ability to enjoy each moment.
-A loss of interest in judging people.
-A loss of interest in judging self.
-A loss of interest in interpreting the actions of others.
-A loss of interest in conflict.
-A loss of the ability to worry.
-Frequent, overwhelming episodes of appreciation.
-Contented feelings of connectedness with others and nature.
-Frequent attacks of smiling.
-An increased tendency to let things happen rather than make them happen.
-An increased susceptibility to the love extended by others as well as the uncontrollable urge to extend it.

Adventurous living, walking the path of joy, is ultimately about dealing with change. Change is inevitable in life. We either embrace it or try to avoid it. Yet change continually happens, whether imposed from outside us, gradually as we respond to life's gentle nudges, or self-directed as we understand and apply basic truth and listen to the "still, small voice within." Change involves transition periods, with losses and gains, and usually isn't comfortable.

A client wrote me the following, which sums up this process of facing challenges and creating change in life. She wrote:

When I was introduced into the program (AA), I was told to "Let Go and Let God." I became furious. "Do you have any idea how hard I had to work to get this far? Do you have any idea how difficult it was? How I always had to speak up for myself? How no one was listening to me?!!!"

And God answered, "But I was listening."

So I have learned I was never alone. Now I am being asked "Can you let go of fear long enough to allow Me fully into your Life? You do not have to fight anymore. That the entire world is being offered to you to take with an open palm and not a fist. Since when have material things become more important to you than what is inside? It is time to re-prioritize your life. Is your home more important to you than yourself? Is your car more important than ME? You are being asked to choose the road you walk upon the rest of your life. Which will it be? The one paved with cars, houses, jewelry and toys or the one paved with Trust, Self-Acceptance, Courage and Love?

For me, I have never preferred the common road. When others have turned right, I have turned left. If most see the mountains at sunset, I wondered what do they look like at sunrise. Therefore, if most look at life from the material perspective, why not try the spiritual. Their road might be paved by bricks but mine, I know, will be paved with Gold.

Joyful living is facing all the challenges, adversities, opportunities and experiences. It is embracing life with an adventurous attitude and approach. It is understanding and applying basic truths, rediscovering our spiritual heritage as we have this human experience. It is taking the path of joy, the path paved with Gold.

Life IS an adventure. Live the adventure fully and completely. Live your adventure. Return to your spiritual heritage, and enjoy your human experience. Embrace life totally, completely and absolutely. As you walk the path of joy you return to your true Self. Manifest your life as a masterpiece of joy. Be joy.

Return to You.

Namaste.

Comparative Book List

Chopra, Deepak (1993) *Ageless Mind, Timeless Body*
New York: Harmony Books
The similarity is in the concept of the power of thought and belief, and the application to physical health. The difference is a broader perspective is taken encompassing many basic truths to create joy.

Dyer, Wayne W. (1992) *Real Magic*
New York: Harper-Collins Publishers
The similarity is in the concept of creating real magic in our lives with the power of thought, and in the blend of psychological and spiritual principles. The book is also about exploring universal truths in more detail, exploring healing, growth and awareness at the physical, mental and emotional levels, and exploring love, the heart-mind connection and service.

Mandino, Og (1995) *The Spellbinder's Gift*
New York: Fawcett Coumbine Books
The similarity is in the simple presentation of spiritual truth in an inspirational manner. The book has a broader examination of topics and truths, and adventurous living.

Peck, M. Scott (1978) *The Road Less Traveled*
New York: A Touchstone Book, published by Simon & Shuster
The similarity is in the presentation of psychological and spiritual principles, the discussion of love and the concept of meeting and facing challenges. The book also has specific universal laws, differing guidelines and approaches to healing, ways of meeting the challenges of life, and a specific understanding of mission and working within the divine plan.

Redfield, James (1993) *The Celestine Prophecy*
Hoover, Alabama: Satori Publishing
The similarity is in the concept of adventure and specific guidelines to spiritual truths. The book also gives guidelines to growth and awareness, and implementation of activities to return to our divine heritage.

ABOUT THE AUTHOR

Eric Alsterberg, Ph.D. is a clinical psychologist licensed to practice in the state of Michigan, where he currently resides. His doctorate in Clinical Psychology is from United States International University in San Diego, California; his undergraduate degree in Education from the University of Michigan, and a Masters Degree in Clinical Psychology from Eastern Michigan University.

A psychotherapist for twenty-seven years, working with both mental health and substance abuse populations, he currently has his own practice, consults to inpatient mental health and substance abuse programs, provides supervision to other clinicians, and provides consultation to outpatient clinics. Dr. Alsterberg has been involved in direct service, custody and visitation evaluations, college teaching, and agency and program management and supervision.

Increasingly, Dr. Alsterberg has expanded the scope of his clinical practice to address spiritual and metaphysical issues, since his clients wanted to discuss and address those issues, as well as more traditional issues, in treatment. In the past four years, he developed a new concept in hypnosis treatment, called "vision hypnosis" or "vision hypnotherapy." This is an extension of regression hypnosis, but involves the emergence of decreased relatives, angels, guardian spirits, archangels, and ascended masters during the hypnotic trance, facilitating further healing work with the client. Visionary experiences also arise, either as metaphors for the client, or glimpses of current or future events in this and other dimensions. He works to provide healing at the physical, mental, emotional and spiritual levels, using "light visualization technologies" and "shamanic" methods as needed. His work has increasingly used "Metaphysical Therapy."